THE RISE OF LULA DARLING

ALEX DEAN

TREBOR AND TAYLOR PUBLISHING

ALSO BY ALEX DEAN

Lula Darling Series

The Secret Life of Lula Darling

A Life's Purpose

The Rise of Lula Darling

Alexis Fields Thrill Series

Restraining Order

The Bogeyman Next Door

Stalked

Alexis Fields - Complete Thrill Series Box Set

Standalone Books

The Client

A High-Stakes Crime Thriller

CHAPTER 1

THE MIRACLE STARTED on West Washington Street, in the courtyard of the Daley Center. I stood on top of a wooden platform, flanked by civil rights activists from around the country and community organizers from far-reaching ends of the city. My mother sat patiently in a chair next to the stage. Also notably present was Pastor E.L. Tompkins of the 1st Deliverance Baptist Church of Bronzeville.

Satisfied with the turnout, I raised my bullhorn to deliver what I'd hoped would be a lasting message. Looking over the racially diverse sea of faces, I immediately addressed my supporters, starting with a series of qualifying questions. "Are you willing to dedicate your life to your cause? Are you willing to dedicate your life to bring forth justice and equality? Are you prepared to leave a better quality of life for your children, your grand-children?" I paused and then smiled as I heard a contingent among them reply and raise their fists in the air.

"*Yes!*"

We were not here demanding any special treatment, only the equal treatment that our country's founders had promised.

I wanted to speak to the hearts of those serious about changing the status quo.

It was a cold but sunny Saturday morning. A new president had been sworn into the Whitehouse, and race relations in U.S. had taken a serious turn for the worse. For roughly an hour I revealed an outline of my plan to bring about real change in this country, starting with my adopted hometown of Chicago. With senseless violence a constant concern, there was no better place that I could think of to dig trenches for a grassroots' effort.

Over the past twelve months, the movement that I'd started had begun to gain traction. And my name had been circulating ever since my boyfriend, Marcus, had unexpectedly introduced me to an audience of millions at last year's Grammy Awards.

The media had referred to what I'd said onstage that night as "The most bodacious, unscheduled, well-timed speech heard around the world."

Marcus had become more and more socially conscious, sometimes putting his aspirations for fame and fortune in the music business on hold to lend his time to the Cause. Even me and my mother's search to find our biological kin after arriving here from the past must have inspired him to finally want to learn more about the family he never knew on his absentee father's side.

As the downtown rally concluded and the PA equipment was put away, a young reporter who told me that he worked for a local African-American online newspaper approached me. I invited him to a gathering being held afterward at the church of Pastor E.L. Tompkins. It was a once-a-month think tank including local clergy and myself, where we would put our resources together, and worked toward raising money for the Cause. But most of all, we worked toward a common goal for the betterment of the people.

My best friend, Ariel, texted me to tell me that she was on her way and that she would meet me, Mama, and Marcus in the Fellowship Hall at the church. Ariel was the Movement's newly appointed treasurer. She was an accountant by day and had been good with numbers ever since we were teenage girls living with her parents. I remember during the summer when her parents allowed her to oversee their monthly financial budget, calculate expenses, and suggest in what areas the family could possibly save money.

Well, Ariel was pregnant now and ready to give birth at any time. So I had pleaded, basically begged her to stay at home. But being the kind-hearted soul that she was, and against the advice of her doctor, she insisted on coming to the meeting to account for donations raised by different ministers who had been participating in the cause. Although, I wondered if it had more to do with the time she accompanied me to church, and as the ushers passed around collection plates, Pastor Tompkins had shouted from the pulpit for them to keep an eye on the money, then added: *'Everybody here don't know Jesus!'*

When we finally emerged in front of the church, a large man with a thick mustache and side-burns came up to my car. He was dressed in a pinstriped maroon suit with a black shirt, a red tie, and on top of his head sat a black fedora. He grinned broadly. "Lula? Are you Lula?" he asked enthusiastically.

"Yes," I replied and smiled back.

"Willie Mack Quarles," he announced, jutting out his hand. "My congregation calls me Pastor Mack. Today was the first chance I had to attend one of these meetings. And I just want to say I'm so proud of what you're doing young lady." He turned to briefly survey the cars filing into 1st Deliverance's parking lot. "Getting all of the churches on one accord like this. That was a very smart move on your part. I listened to your speech down at the Daley Center today. I must say that you seem wise above your years. What we old folks like to call an old soul."

"Thank you!" I replied as we began walking through the parking lot. "I know that once all of the churches are onboard with the Movement, we can begin pressing for some serious change. As history has taught us, without a doubt, there is great power in numbers."

Pastor Mack nodded. "Oh, absolutely, and I pray that God makes a way; I pray that he makes this goal of ours a reality. For there's power in prayer, too!" He opened the door to the church, and Marcus and I followed a line of people through

the sanctuary and down a set of stairs into Fellowship Hall.

In the center of the room, there was a long
table covered with a white linen cloth. On top of
it were plastic utensils, cups, napkins, all placed
there by Mrs. Mary Wiggins, who also happened
to be the church's proverbial cook. She was
wearing a white apron and wore plastic gloves and
a hair net. Her buttermilk fried chicken and real
mashed potatoes could put most restaurants to
shame, and everyone who had come to know her
personally, especially those blessed to have
sampled her great cooking, affectionately called
her Ms. Mary.

We gathered around the table where different
ministers from around the city emptied envelopes
filled with cash, checks, and money orders. Ms.
Mary came in with a cold pitcher of iced tea and
filled everyone's cups. Pastor Tompkins came in the
room holding some type of accounting form and sat
at the end of the table. "From the looks of it, we've
raised a generous amount this month. Congratulations, gentlemen, and ladies," he said.

The young reporter who I'd invited from the
newspaper quickly raised his hand. "Pastor Tompkins, if you don't mind me asking, for my write up,

can you explain what will be done with the money raised?"

Pastor Tompkins clasped his hands in front of him. "Sure, that's a good and meaningful question. Some of it will go toward spreading the word in the media, including on social media. Some of it will go toward our website, which will be used for more fundraising. But the majority of it will go toward Lula's ultimate goal of structuring a—"

"Help her into a chair!"

My gaze cut away from Pastor Tomkins. I glanced up and saw Ariel, one hand on her waist, wobbling through the doorway. Marcus and I immediately stood and helped my friend get settled into a seat. "Sorry I'm late," She announced as she gently lowered herself into the chair. "I was up late last night. So I'm moving a little slow this morning. But I didn't want to miss the meeting."

Pastor Mack nodded and cracked a grin. "Come hell or high water, huh? Now that's what I call dedication!" he exclaimed, his voice husky and low. "Now if only my ex-wife had been that dedicated."

Everyone at the table, including Ariel, laughed. "Wishful thinking," I said, standing up grinning. Then I got up and gathered all of the checks, the money orders, the cash, and put the Movement's donations directly in front of her. She opened a folder and took out some accounting forms that she had brought from her job. Then she took out a financial calculator from her purse and began adding.

Ms. Mary rolled out a steel service cart from the church's kitchen. It had three levels and was filled with large oval platters of food. "All right, everybody. Get ready to eat while the food is still hot," she announced as she pushed the cart forward while setting plates on the table. It had been our usual habit of eating before we actually got down to talking business. Seeing the camaraderie among these pastors, their laughter, seeing Ms. Mary pushing that serving cart, made me think of something I once saw on TV. I think it was the White House Correspondents' dinner before President Obama had left office.

Ms. Mary arrived where I was seated. But before she could set a plate in front of me, there was a piercing scream coming from my left so loud my heart almost leaped from my chest. Ms. Mary dropped a set of oven mitts she'd had in her hand. I turned and saw Ariel holding her stomach. "I think it's time!" she gasped. Marcus and I pulled back her chair from the table. "Quick, get her into E.L.'s office. There's a couch in there," Ms. Mary blurted. With Ariel standing, one of her arms over Marcus's shoulder and the other around mine, we followed Pastor Tompkins and escorted her into his office. "I'll call an ambulance," he said.

We got Ariel settled down against the back of the sofa. Marcus and Pastor Tompkins left the room as Ms. Mary, and I took over. Ms. Mary grabbed several towels that had been resting on her shoulder. "I used to work as a home caregiver for seniors in my younger years. Although I wasn't delivering babies, the elderly clients I saw everyday needed just as much care and attention." Ms. Mary leaned over. Her eyes were wide like half-moons. "Don't panic, either one of you. Should that baby enter this world before the ambulance gets here, just follow my lead," she said. "But first, I'm going to need some warm water, more towels, and something to cover this couch with."

I nodded, then rushed into the hallway and grabbed some towels and a plastic tablecloth from a storage closet. Then I went into the church's kitchen and filled up a large pot I saw sitting on the counter. When I returned, I set the pot on the floor and handed Ms. Mary the towels and plastic. Then

I watched her as she prepared to go to work. My neck flushed with heat.

Ariel held her stomach and belted out a massive groan. Ms. Mary raised Ariel's dress higher up on her torso. "Just relax and push!" Mary used her elbows to keep Ariel's legs apart and then reached forward. Ariel squinted her eyes shut and took deep breaths to cope with the obvious pain.

Several minutes later the round knob of a head had appeared, then slowly, the rest of the baby's body. "It's a boy!" I blurted. Ms. Mary settled the baby on top of the tablecloth and towels that she'd laid on the couch. He was covered with an ample amount of blood and fluid. I stood there and watched with joy and amazement, because this was the first time I'd ever seen a live birth. With his eyes closed, the baby jerked his arms and legs, struggling for his first cry. Then he peered at the ceiling's fluorescent light before belting out his first scream.

I ran from the room to get more clean towels and a blanket. When I returned, Ms. Mary and I knelt at the end of the couch and cleaned the baby's body. Ariel smiled and reached out her arms as her forehead beaded with sweat. Ms. Mary gently raised the infant as Ariel set him on her chest.

"Look at you, Thomas Rayome Jr.," she murmured as she affectionately stared at her newborn.

"Isn't he the most precious thing," I said, gazing down at the baby as Ariel cradled him. Ms. Mary stood up and rested her hands on her hips. "He sure is, and looks as healthy as can be, to my untrained eye, anyway."

Suddenly there was a knock on the door. I got up to open it as Ms. Mary shielded Ariel with the blanket. It was Pastor Tompkins notifying us that the paramedics were here. So I pulled the door all the way open, and the medics came in with a steel gurney, its wheels clacking as they rolled it over the carpet.

As I watched Ariel bond with her new baby boy, I couldn't help but think that today was the start of several life-changing events all at once. One, my best friend, who was also like a sister, had given birth, a real blessing in and of itself. But on top of that, everything I'd ever dreamed of accomplishing with the Movement had finally started to happen.

I began to feel more empowered. More confident in my ability to lead. And that I was being guided by a force much greater than I could have ever imagined. Whatever the case may be—I was now, more than ever—ready to be a godmother to

Ariel's son. Ready to help him know what to say when he asks a girl out on a date or asks a girl to go to the prom, or how to wisely navigate the choppy waters of life. For all this and more I wanted to be there for him. And be a beacon of hope to a suffering people.

CHAPTER 2

THE FIRST TIME I stepped into Pastor Tompkins' church was exhilarating. I remember the moment when Mama and I had entered the sanctuary, finally being able to feel secure in our faith, being able to express our feelings for God without cowering in fear, or persecution. These feelings, I imagined, were like everything that most people nowadays had taken for granted.

To move matters forward, Pastor Tompkins had provided me with a list of other pastors and clergy whom he knew personally. I contacted each one of them, sometimes through their secretaries, or board members, and scheduled meetings each day after work. Marcus, who had thousands of friends on Facebook, had helped me to spread the word on social media.

Ariel had taken a course on web design, which was paid for by the company she now worked for. She ended up designing the website for the Movement. It looked professionally done, with pages of articles and photos of movements past and present, attacks on people of color by white supremacists, and shootings of unarmed minorities by the police. Anyone interested in joining the cause could register to be notified of matters of importance, along with being able to sign petitions via an online submission form.

The last minister that I had been scheduled to meet with was located in a somewhat revitalized area on the West Side. Our meeting was for 4 p.m., and I had arrived roughly seven minutes beforehand. I had heard that he was well connected politically and that he could make things happen with a simple phone call. I'd also heard some unflattering things about him through the grapevine, like his primary motivation for showing up on Sundays wasn't necessarily to save souls. But to line his pockets with what Mama and I had learned was called the Prosperity Gospel.

I had absolutely no problem with anyone being prosperous. In fact, that was part of what the Movement was about, helping those at an economic disadvantage. But I felt that anyone who called himself a servant of God should preach on *all* of what the good book had to say, and not just parts of it. Ironically, on top of that, the pastor's name I'd been told was Ezekiel Fortune.

I sat in my car for several minutes listening to the radio where a DJ had been talking about Janet Jackson's most recent concert. On the corner there was a group of men huddled, talking. Then a homeless man approached my car with a bottle of liquid in one hand and a small towel in the other. He had matted hair, a weather-beaten face and was wearing tattered clothes. "Need your windshield washed? I'll make it clean as new," he said and smiled. I shook my head. It took several responses of no and me shaking my head before I slightly lowered the window and handed him a five-dollar bill. After that, he finally moved along. Several minutes later, I got out of my car and opened the door to the church. It looked like I had immediately been transformed into another, more affluent community. The interior, from expensive looking artwork that adorned the walls, to the shiny floor tile and fancy lighting, was the complete opposite of how things had looked on the outside. A woman sitting in a small office saw me come in and rose from her desk. She walked into the foyer.

"May I help you?" She didn't smile. She looked wary of probably anyone who had stepped through the church's door outside of Sunday.

"Yes, ma'am. I'm Lula Darling. I have a 4 p.m. meeting with Pastor Fortune?"

She looked me up and down, then jerked her head. "You can follow me."

I trailed her around a corner and into a large office where a man was seated in a leather chair. He was watching a video of a sermon on a flat screen that sat on an entertainment shelf. The audio was extremely loud. He spun his chair around. He looked surprisingly young, notwithstanding the streaks of gray shot through his hair. He was dressed impeccably and had rings on three of the fingers on each of his hands. He smiled and then grabbed the TV's remote to turn it down.

He leaned forward over his desk. "I presume you're the young lady who requested a meeting with me? Glad to meet you. Please, have a seat." He pointed to a chair directly in front of his cherry wood desk. "Well, I'm pastor Fortune." He glanced at his watch. "And I don't mean to be rude, but I have like, only twenty minutes before I have to leave for a dinner engagement. What can I do for you?"

I briefly looked past his gaze and noticed pictures on the bookshelf behind him of he and the mayor shaking hands. There were also pictures of him with several celebrities, including some world-renowned gospel artists.

"Thank you for meeting with me. I won't take up a lot of your time. Let me get straight to the point. I'm an activist who has started a movement to change things in this country. To make it right and better for the disadvantaged among us, the downtrodden. So, to do that, I plan to gather large masses of people, organize boycotts, and put pressure on the powers that be to do right by us. There is strength in numbers, Mr. Fortune." I pulled from my purse a sheet of statistical data to illustrate my point. "Did you know that we as a people have a documented buying power of 1.3 Trillion? And that number continues to increase." Pastor Fortune reached out to receive the paper, which I enthusiastically handed him across the desk. "Refusing to buy their products could economically cripple big corporations almost overnight. But my first order of business is to get all of the churches onboard. Because once the churches are in accord, I know that the Movement will take on a life of its own. A lot of churches of different denominations and ministers in Chicago are already interested and are now taking part in our efforts. We're starting to see places of worship from other states get involved, too."

Pastor Fortune glanced up from studying the sheet of paper I had given him. Then he leaned back in his chair and exhaled deeply. "I can't do this," he explained.

I shrugged. I struggled to find a diplomatic way to handle the rest of the conversation without being politely escorted from the building. Suddenly I sensed a seismic shift between us. "Why?"

"Well, because—"

"Because?" I repeated, pressing for the reason behind his reluctance.

He leaned forward and clasped his hands in front of him. "Because, if I can be totally honest with you . . . your idea of bringing about economic change doesn't align with that of the church's. Besides, if the church becomes politically active like you're suggesting, there might be retribution."

"How do you mean?"

Pastor Fortune shook his head. "You don't get it, do you? Everything in this world is political whether we want to realize it or not. If the church becomes antiestablishment, the next thing you know they'll probably try to take our tax-exempt status away. Most churches in America have organized as 501c3 tax-exempt religious organizations. And I'm sure I speak for most of them when I say we'd like to keep it that way."

I shook my head. "See, that is exactly the problem," I countered. "We need to be willing to sacrifice for any change to occur. Just like our forefathers did to allow you and I the opportunities and the money that we have today. We can't keep doing the same things over and over and expect to get different results!"

Pastor Fortune furrowed his brow and his eyes locked on mine in a whirl of astonishment. He probably wondered how such a young woman of color had the absolute gall and audacity to come into his office spewing such bodacious ideas. He looked quite uneasy now.

"It's taken years to build this church to where it is today. I'll tell you what, though," he said as he pulled out a drawer from his desk. "If you can show me where the money you've collected is going, and how it's benefitting the poor communities of Chicago, I will donate a nice amount to your cause.

Mainly because I feel it's the right thing to do. And the fact that my good friend, Pastor Mack, is helping you doesn't hurt either. But I don't want either my name or the church's name associated with your movement."

I stood from my chair and reached forward as he handed me his business card. "Thank you. I'll have our accountant provide you with the necessary details about the Movement's financial transactions."

He nodded. "I'll look forward to it. In the meantime, I pray that God keeps you and that he blesses your efforts."

Pastor Fortune pressed a button on his phone and summoned his secretary to accompany me on my way out. As I left the building, I thought about how my meetings with local pastors and the ensuing organized boycotts were already proving to be more effective than any street marches or protests. Collectively, we were becoming a conscious threat.

CHAPTER 3

ON THE FOLLOWING DAY, I left L. Bowers Elementary and headed downtown to a meeting with
Detective Ryan Laurence, whom Ariel and I had
met after the turbulent night of protests on
Michigan Avenue. The first time I called him and
told him what I'd wanted: To meet with whatever
documented gang member was mostly in charge of
the South Side's Englewood neighborhood, he
thought I had completely lost my mind.

To my surprise, he had agreed to do it. But only
on the condition that the meeting was held at police
headquarters on 35th and South Michigan. He had
also suggested that I use an alias to ensure some
degree of anonymity, for my safety. Although that
was becoming increasingly harder due to my
continuous exposure in the media.

When I arrived at the station, I was led into a room that looked much like the kind you saw on TV during intense police interrogations, only slightly larger. There was a grey table, several chairs, a mirror on the wall. Already seated was a young man with a smooth bronze complexion, narrow face, thin mustache, and three tatted teardrops on the left side of his face. He trained his eyes on me as I entered the room.

"Taisha?" the cop lied as he addressed me. "This here is Larone Toobin, known on the street as L.T. He's currently in custody on drug and weapons charges. Has an upcoming hearing in two weeks, but has agreed to cooperate with your organization in exchange for the possibility of getting a reduced sentence. My plan is to hand over the request to the State's Attorney's office within forty-eight hours."

I quickly shifted my gaze from Detective Laurence to the gang leader who sat opposite me on the other side of the table.

He jerked his chin. "Wassup?"

"Hi," I responded nervously. For a brief moment, I thought about Jodie Foster's character, Clarice Starling when she went to meet Hannibal Lecter in *Silence of the Lambs*. I'd seen it at least three times since it was one of Ariel's favorite movies to pull from her DVD collection whenever she was either bored or during one of the frequent breakups between her and her boyfriend, Tommy. I also knew that the tear-shaped tats beneath Toobin's left eye supposedly meant that he'd killed at least three people.

There was no other choice but for me to come on strong, direct. "I need your help," I said sharply. "I've got a movement to help the least of our people overcome the conditions they find themselves in, overcome institutionalized racism, injustice where applicable. It requires that all gangs in this city and hopefully more, stop the killing."

Toobin leaned back in his chair and smirked. "What's it to you? Shouldn't you be somewhere shakin' your butt in a club instead of worrying about racism and injustice?"

Detective Laurence interjected. "It's none of your concern where she shakes her ass or why she's doing what she's doing. Your only concern should be to help her; you know what I'm saying? If not, the deal for leniency is off the table."

Toobin glanced up. "Say's who?"

Detective Laurence pulled out a chair and

forcefully slapped a manila folder on top of the table. "Say's me. With your record, and the new laws in place for repeat offenders, you'll be going away for a long time, dude."

The gang member swiveled his gaze toward me. "I want you to put the word on the streets that the killing has to stop. Working collectively, we can implement a plan to bring jobs and other economic opportunities to our communities, where this life of crime the gangs engage in will eventually be a thing of the past," I told him.

Toobin paused for a moment, then shook his head. "Hell nah. No way. Y'all crazy if you think that's gonna happen!"

"I want to make life easier for you. I want to help lighten your sentence. Do you have any children?" I asked him.

"Yeah, I got three."

"You want them growing up following in your footsteps, possibly getting shot before they make it to being a teenager?" I asked. "Or do you want them to have a chance in life, like the kids on the affluent North Side, or in the suburbs. They live in a whole other world, in case you haven't noticed, despite it being only minutes away. Why can't you and *your* children, and your family, have the same?"

Toobin cocked his head. He raised his cuffed hands on top of the table, the steel links rattling as he did so. He furrowed his left brow and pointed a finger at me, then at Detective Laurence. " All right, if I do what y'all want me to do? I want round the clock protection while I'm in this rat hole and *if and when* I go to prison. Because once word gets out that I'm cooperating with y'all, I might as well be planning my homegoing."

Detective Laurence drew in a deep breath. "Smart man," he said.

I smiled and reached across the table to shake Toobin's shackled hand. Although I had remained anonymous by name, I was still concerned with the fact that this man had already seen my face. It was only a little past the half-year mark, and Chicago had already racked up enough murders to surpass last year's total. Most of it I'd been told was either gang or drug-related. So here I was in this closed off interrogation room sitting across from one of the city's most notorious gang members, getting myself involved ever so deeply. But if it meant making a difference in the number of homicides and stopping the bloodshed, I would not have wanted to be anywhere else. "I'm going to give you a plan of action to give to the members of your gang," I told him. "My organization will be working with them starting first thing next Monday at a Southside location, which will be disclosed later. You need to assure them that life as they know it has come to an end."

CHAPTER 4

AGAINST HER PARENTS' wishes, and after many nights of disagreements, Ariel and Tommy had started living together. After six long weeks of looking for a two-bedroom apartment, they had finally found a place in the West Loop. Once they got settled and had furnished their place, they invited their closest friends and family over for a housewarming. Mama and I had received our invitation and were on our way with a Keurig we'd purchased as a gift from Walmart.

Throughout the whole process, Tommy had been impatient about moving. He could have cared less *where* they lived. He seemed to have gotten more insecure now that Ariel had taken a high paying job, and wanted to keep tabs on her. My best friend had confided in me one night during one of our weekly phone conversations that their move had taken a month and a half for several good reasons. First, Ariel wanted to be close to good daycare when the time was right for her son to start school. Second, her parents were not pleased that she'd decided to shack up with her son's father, especially without any firm plans of marriage on the horizon. They wanted her to take her time—carefully consider the move she was making. "There was no rush or pressure to leave," they had assured her.

Although her parents considered themselves proudly progressive and liberal, they still held on to good old-fashion ideals when it came to their daughter. Their one and only child.

Like any parent, they only wanted the best for her.

Then there was the fact that her father had never cared much for Tommy, which meant that Ariel went out of her way to limit as much interaction as possible between the two of them. In fact, ever since I'd known her, I cannot ever remember a time when Tommy had actually set foot in Ariel's house. The closest he had ever gotten was to the door of their condo when he called from his cell phone from an elevator to tell her that she'd forgotten her purse in his car.

Mama and I arrived just before six and had parked several blocks away. The skies were beginning to darken, and only a few people were outside, a woman walking her dog, a man with earbuds, jogging.

When we entered the apartment, I immediately saw people I did not recognize. The place was extremely well decorated. There was a gray sectional in the living room, a glass and metal entertainment against the front wall and cream-colored vertical blinds covering the front window. It was very apparent that Ariel had inherited her mother's knack for good decorating. Several women hugged her as they each held a glass of wine. Tommy was waltzing around between the kitchen and living room showing off their son. A group of older people who I believed were Ariel's relatives from Wisconsin had been locked in conversation regarding the reality TV star in the White House. Mama and I said hello, sat our gift on the table in the kitchen, and then took a seat on the couch.

Almost immediately, a man came over to where Mama and I sat and introduced himself as, Ron, Ariel's uncle. Ariel had previously told me about most of her family, including how Ron had been deployed for two tours in Iraq, only to find out that his wife was abruptly leaving him for another man. It had happened right before Christmas. She didn't even have the decency to tell him when he came home on leave. After that, Ariel had said, "he'd spent every evening for two and a half months drowning out his sorrows by drinking a fifth of Jack Daniels."

"And you must be, Lula?" He said, extending his hand.

"Yes, pleased to meet you." I smiled cordially. "And seated next to me is my mother, Ella Mae."

Ron nodded and took a sip from the small glass he was holding. "Nice to meet you both." He gestured toward the door. "It would have also been nice if my brother and sister-in-law were not late and stuck in traffic. They texted me several minutes ago saying that they were on their way. In the meantime—on behalf of my lovely niece, please, make yourselves at home."

Ron milled around the apartment greeting other guests, as "I Feel It Coming" by The Weeknd played low in the background. Shortly after, Ariel and Tommy came over to greet us. She had their son gently cradled in her arms.

"This is a nice place you both have," Mama and I said in unison.

Ariel beamed. "Thank you. We're not far from my job, which is a plus. And this little bugger's daycare is right around the corner." The baby started crying, kicking his legs as if on an imaginary bicycle and windmilling his arms in frustration. Ariel muttered a gentle shush, then excused herself and walked into the kitchen to grab a bottle.

Tommy trailed Ariel with his gaze as she left the room. "Yeah, it's a major upgrade, a far cry from the dump *I* called home several weeks ago," he said. "Everything's a short walking distance from here. The only thing I'm missing is being able to turn up my surround sound like I want." He smiled. "I *definitely* don't want to be the cause of us being thrown out of here. By the way, where's Marcus?"

"He couldn't make it. He had some big music project going on at the studio." Knowing how close Marcus and Tommy had been, it was surprising to see that Tommy didn't know what Marcus had been up to, either professionally, or personally. I tilted my head, confused. "What . . . he didn't tell you?"

Tommy shook his head and shrugged. "No, actually I haven't talked to him since we moved."

Suddenly there was some loud talking and commotion at the door. I turned and saw Ariel's parents coming in the apartment holding several bags of groceries. Her uncle Ron rushed over to grab a heavy bag that her mother was carrying. Ariel gave the baby to Tommy to hold. Then she strolled around the room introducing her parents to a few of her coworkers. I saw her father glance briefly at Tommy with a look of disdain. After putting away some things in the refrigerator and into cabinets, Ariel's mother, Patty, came waltzing into the living room. Her face was thick with foundation. Her hair a different shade of brown since the last time I'd seen her. It spilled toward the base of her neck, curved upward to just above her shoulders. She smiled, revealing small web works of lines around the eyes. "Lula, Ella Mae, glad you could make it this evening." She glanced at me and Mama wide-eyed, her hands balanced on her hips. "So, looks like our only child has left the nest to strike out on her own."

I nodded and smiled. "It was bound to happen sooner or later. And I'm very proud of her and Tommy. Now I'm looking forward to a destination wedding with amazing beaches and fantastic food!"

Tommy brought the baby back in the room. Thomas Jr. was nursing his bottle as Tommy handed him back to Ariel. After settling the baby in the nook of her arm, she cocked her head and then chuckled. "Um . . . and *I'm* the one who supposedly can't keep a secret? But yeah, my parents already know it's my dream to have a destination wedding in either Acapulco or Puerto Vallarta—thank you very much!"

"So when's the date?" Mama asked.

Tommy shrugged. "Well, I told Ariel that before anybody starts talking about marriage, the first thing they've got to do is have their finances in order. And to be honest, Ms. Darling, we ain't there yet."

Suddenly Ariel's father appeared from the kitchen holding a can of Coors light. "Did I overhear my baby girl talking about a wedding date?" He looked at his wife then at Ariel and Tommy. "So, when is it? When do I get to give my daughter away?"

"In due time, Mr. Evans. We don't want to rush, or take our vows lightly." Tommy smiled. "I'm sure you can understand that, right?"

Ariel's father took a sip from his beer. "Nope, actually I don't."

"*Dad!*" Ariel exploded.

"No, Ariel, I think it's about time he hears this. I can no longer remain silent about this at the expense of being politically correct." Ariel's dad looked at Tommy with disgust. "You know . . . I never really warmed up to you, Tommy. But you're whom my little girl chose, and I have come to terms with that. I accept it. However, her getting pregnant —in my opinion—is a game changer. So I say it's time to stop being vague about what your real intentions are and step up to the plate. Like a man is supposed to do."

The baby started crying almost as if he'd somehow sensed the tension afloat. Ariel's mother shot her husband a glare and then promptly decided to grasp his arm. "Honey, this isn't the time. We have guests here, and more importantly, this is their housewarming. Let's deal with this at a more appropriate time."

Ariel's father turned and walked into the kitchen. Then her uncle sauntered over—spinning himself around as he made his way toward us. "You folks act like you're at a frickin funeral." He stumbled to one side as he raised his drink in the air. "My niece and her boyfriend have just moved in together," he said waving his arms. "This is cause for a *celebration!* Is it not? Or did I end up in the wrong apartment?"

"Tell that to my father. He seems absolutely *intent* on ruining everything," Ariel snapped. Ron looked back at his brother, who simply smiled and raised his beer. He nodded and winked as if giving a symbolic toast from across the room. I imagined that my friend had to have been embarrassed by the friction between her boyfriend and her father. As we sat cordially on the couch, I wondered if things would take a turn for the worse. I hoped that the answer was no. Mama and I had definitely seen enough drama to last us another lifetime.

Ariel then handed off her baby to one of her aunts from Wisconsin. Her name was Gertie. Ariel said that Gertie had lived alone and had been married once to a man with a terrible gambling addiction. Over a period of five years, they had lost everything, all of their assets including a forty-acre organic dairy farm. She had no kids of her own. And she had always been the type to pretend that her life was perfect while pointing out the dysfunction in everyone else's.

"He's got those same little puffy red cheeks that you had when you were a baby, Ariel," Gertie muttered as she stared down at Thomas Jr. The baby started crying again, and Ariel reached out her arms to receive him. Then she took him into the bedroom to change his diaper.

Gertie clasped her hands in her lap and then

glanced up at me. "Lula, am I pronouncing your name right?"

I nodded. "Yes, ma'am."

"I saw Ariel post on Facebook that her best friend was the victim of a drive-by shooting. That was you, am I correct?"

The last thing I wanted was to relive the nightmare of that day. And I wondered why Ariel's aunt would feel the need to bring that up now. *Here. Tonight*, of all places. I simply wanted to enjoy my friend's housewarming.

I exhaled. "Yes, that's correct."

Gertie's face contorted. "Oh, how awful," she said, shaking her head. "That must have been downright terrifying."

"It was. I'm just thankful that I wasn't harmed. And that I'm still alive to even talk about it," I said.

Gertie shook her head. "I couldn't imagine the horror you must have felt." Then she reached over and gently clapped a hand on my knee. "Well, I'm just glad to see that you are okay. We get Chicago news up in Wisconsin where I live, and . . . it just seems to be getting worse everywhere."

I was grateful to hear what sounded like genuine concern. Although I couldn't imagine that Ariel's aunt would even know what it was like to live in

Chicago, let alone, living with a constant concern for her safety like I had to do. It's amazing how sometimes people from entirely different backgrounds and upbringings can cross each other's paths. Perhaps it was God's way of showing us that despite our differences in schooling, money and skin color, there was still more we had in common than not. Like the desire to live in safe neighborhoods—and certain hopes for America's future.

Ariel and Tommy returned from the bedroom. Ariel was holding a photo album while Tommy held their son. I could tell from the smirk on her face that she was up to something.

"So, I've got some pictures of Lula that are hilarious."

"Pictures of what? You've got pictures of me?" I asked.

Ariel nodded. "Yes. I do, Lula. I took them with my cell phone when we went to Six Flags Great America."

"I can't believe you did this!" I said, beaming.

Ariel leaned over and lay open the photo album between my lap and Mama's. "I snapped two shots as the roller coaster dropped like a stone." She pointed. "Now is that *funny* or what?"

Mama and I burst out laughing. This had to be

the absolutely most embarrassing image that I had ever seen of myself. In the photo, my hair was standing up on end, pointed straight to the sky as if I'd been hit with a megawatt jolt of electricity. My face was contorted, my eyes wide, like that of a person instantly met with an extreme circumstance of shock and horror.

But with all that was going on in the world and in my own life, I truly treasured moments like this. I cherished the chance to be around my family, to be around my friends, to have fun despite the enormous responsibility of my life's work.

I cherished the moments...

To just be.

CHAPTER 5

By the end of the week, there was a huge meeting at one of the largest churches in the Auburn Gresham neighborhood on the city's South Side. I was hosting it along with the church's board, which had been heavily involved in the needs and wants of the people who lived in the community. On top of all that, and to my surprise, was Pastor Tompkins. He'd had a renewed interest and a grassroots approach to helping young men and boys who had fallen away from doing anything even remotely positive with their lives.

Ariel and Tommy, Mama, Marcus, and Mama D. had made it a point to be here this evening. Tommy had gone so far as to call in sick from work. If I'd known he'd planned to be here, I would have tried to talk him out of it. Now my concern was with all the media attention, he'd be seen on camera and would have to pay the price for it.

As we pulled up to the concrete steps of the church, I immediately took in its massive castle-like exterior and sweeping architecture. It looked almost mythic as it reached toward the sky against a palette of various shades of blue embedded within the darkening void of space. Then my gaze was quickly drawn to the telescopic antennas atop a line of news vans parked curbside. Every local station was here. Several women who looked like assignment reporters swiped at their hair as they stood on the church's steps.

Marcus got out first and then opened the door of our Chevy Tahoe, which had been graciously provided to us courtesy of the church's board of trustees. I assisted my mother out of the truck while Marcus assisted his grandmother. As I helped Mama outside onto the concrete walkway, pulling up directly behind us was a stretch black limousine. I knew from talking to Marcus and from the partially lowered limo's window that it was his mentor, the rap impresario, Jay Killa, sitting inside.

He stepped out onto the pavement dressed in a crisp black suit and a black turtleneck, talking endlessly to someone on his cell phone. Then he pressed his phone's screen to apparently end the call. "Marcus, Lula, thanks for inviting me to this worthy cause," he said as he took turns embracing us.

I smiled. "No. We actually should be thanking *you*, Jay. For lending your influence and your platform to the Movement."

Jay Killa shrugged. "Y'all don't have to thank me. I'm gonna always be my brother's keeper. Music is just a vessel to allow me to do what's really important."

Before he could take several steps to enter the church, one of the female reporters quickly blocked our path.

"Ms. Darling, what course of action do you intend on addressing during today's summit?"

I glanced up at her. "That's not something I care to comment on at this time," I said. "There's still work that has to be done before disclosing what our future plans are."

She and several more reporters turned their attention to Jay. They immediately swarmed around him like bees around a jar of honey.

"Jay Killa, welcome back to the Windy City! Wendy Kottke, channel seven Eyewitness News. What brings you here to the summit today?"

Killa slowly removed his sunglasses, pinning the reporter with his gaze. "You really want to know the truth?" he said shaking his head. "I'm tired of seeing brothas killing one another. Having spent part of my childhood in Chicago, watching the city and everything that's been going on . . . it strikes me at my very core." He looked down the block and shook his head. "I mean like there was a nine-year-old kid assassinated in an alley last summer! That is insane. All of this madness has got to stop. So I wanted to show up to do whatever I could."

Killa then moved forward and began walking up the church's steps. The five of us followed directly behind him and his entourage through two large wooden doors into a tiled hallway. Marcus glanced over at me. "Mama D. has to go to the washroom. We'll catch up with you all shortly."

I nodded. "Okay." I thought about Mama D.'s health and how after her stint in the hospital, after what the doctor had told her, it appeared that her kidneys were failing now. I believe that Marcus had been in denial about her health. But he also thought about canceling his upcoming tour to make sure she followed the diet her doctor had recommended. Because if the disease worsened, she would be looking at dialysis or perhaps amputation.

Sitting directly on our right on a cloth-draped table was a large white board with a famous quote from Dr. Martin Luther King Jr. And underneath the words was an arrow pointing toward the meeting room where everyone had filed into. As we entered ourselves, I noticed ten long brown conference tables lined across the room, two separate rows of them facing opposite sides. It looked like a setting for a great political debate. In addition to clergy, community activists, and local politicians, there were also several operators of an anti-violence group whose mission was to defuse neighborhood conflicts before they erupted into violence.

I'd also been told that representatives from several major corporations, which had been targeted in our boycott, would be here too. I took that as a victory. No sooner than we could sit though, a middle-aged white man approached our table.

"I recognized this phenomenal young lady instantly. Father Timothy Bigos," he said as he held out a hand to greet me. "I'm the church's senior pastor and wanted to personally thank you and your team, Lula, for helping arrange this important event."

I nodded. "Nice to meet your acquaintance,

Father. And thank you for all the work that you do in the community. And for allowing us to use your church today."

Bigos winced as he glanced around the room. "Well, I'm hoping, and *praying*, that things will work out, and that we can get started without a hitch."

I stared at him, dumbfounded. "What do you mean? Is there a problem?" I asked.

"There are members of several rival gangs here. They were invited. But they'd promised us a truce for at least a day to discuss how we could all work together for the common good of the community. The off-duty Chicago police officers that I normally hire for security are not here yet. My assistant mistakenly gave them the wrong starting time. Now, there's already been a war of words between two high-ranking members of one gang and one high-ranking member of the other." Father Bigos continued. "If things don't simmer down, Lula, I'm afraid I'll have to cancel the summit. And as you may very well know, there seems to be no respect even for houses of worship these days."

I peered around the room. No one here even remotely looked like they would have ever committed a crime, let alone be considered a documented gang member.

I looked back at Father Bigos. "Where are they? I don't see them?"

"They're in the hallway. When I made it known to my staff that there was a threat of violence brewing, Jay Killa, the rapper, said that he would ask them to step outside so that he could talk to them."

"I'll do whatever *I* can to make sure there's not a problem, Father," I said. Then I started making my rounds. I began handing out copies of an outline I'd made of everything that needed to be accomplished for the Movement to be successful. I'd also indicated by what date I expected each of our goals to be completed. I'd spent the last three nights running on two hours sleep just to put my thoughts down on paper.

Pastor Tompkins got up from his chair and helped Marcus assist Mama D. in settling into her seat. She was sitting directly in front of the doorway. I'm sure it was for easy access to the hallway in case she'd needed to go to the bathroom. In my humble opinion, she did not look well. Guilt swelled within my conscious for encouraging her to be here. Her face and her forehead began to glisten with sweat. She immediately opened her purse, then pulled out a copy of *Our Daily Bread* and started fanning herself.

Father Bigos and Pastor Tompkins stood near the front of the room. "We'll get started in a few minutes," Pastor Tompkins announced. "So I'd like to start with a prayer if that's okay with everyone."

Everyone nodded at this. And then we gave God his due. Afterward, there was a brief pause as I reached down into my carrying bag to get a pen and some paper.

"Yes, may we help you, gentlemen?" Father Bigos called out.

I looked up to see whom he was talking to.

And then my whole world came crashing down.

"FBI," one of them blurted and identified himself as the lead agent. There was another agent flanked by two police officers standing at the entrance of the room. One pulled his Windbreaker to the side, revealing the shield on his waist. "Official government business." He nodded in my direction. "We need to have a word with Ms. Lula Darling."

Father Bigos looked at me, then at Pastor Tompkins. You could see the angst on his face as he wondered what was going on. Mama D. struggled to get up. "What in God's name do you want with her? What did she do?"

The FBI agents walked to the side of the room and immediately came toward me.

"Ms. Darling, I'm going to need you to turn around, put your hands behind your back."

I winced. "Ouch." The handcuffs placed over my hands might as well have been circular saws cutting my wrists.

Mama got up and yelled, "You can't arrest her! You have no right!"

Pastor Tompkins attempted to restrain my mother. Then he started approaching, pointing his finger. "This is an injustice! And this is exactly one of the reasons why we're here, today. You can't arrest her and just take her away when she hasn't done anything wrong!"

"Well, we beg to differ," the lead agent countered. I heard the very last click of the cuffs on my wrists. I imagined that they couldn't possibly get any tighter. "Ms. Darling, you've been identified by the FBI as a Black Identity Extremist. A likely threat to both national security and to law enforcement."

Marcus and Ariel stood side by side, forming a human roadblock. But the agents quickly moved them out of the way. Then they began escorting me out of the room. Marcus and Ariel walked along my side as we went down the corridor. It seemed like the longest walk of my life—like I was already a dead woman walking into an unknown fate. "Man, this is my girl. She ain't no threat. She's just trying to *help* people, trying to get justice and equal treatment for all!" The agents ignored Marcus's pleas and hauled me through the wooden doors of the church, down its concrete steps and into a black SUV.

The media was still outside. Several reporters with cameramen in tow rushed over to film me during my arrest. This time I completely ignored their questions. But my entire world was shattered when to my right, I saw a young, maybe five or six-year-old girl staring at me pensively while holding the hand of what looked like her grandmother. And beside them was a group of neighborhood residents taking pictures, and possibly video, with their cell phones.

Right before I was placed in the backseat, I saw Ariel pulling her cell phone out of her purse. "I'm calling my dad!" Tears fell from her cheeks as she held the black railing of the megachurch's steps. I saw Jay Killa come outside, followed by the other agents and the two police officers. He was trying his best to console everyone, probably encouraging them to handle things the right way, and not to make this worse than it already had been.

As the SUV pulled away, I thought about the life of Dr. Martin Luther King Jr. and all of the civil rights leaders that had to climb the hills of adversity to get us where we were today. I thought about how, often when progress was made, it came at the expense of troubling trials and tribulations— even death—to see change being brought to light.

"Where are you taking me?" I asked. One of the agents turned his body in my direction from the front seat. "35th and Michigan. You'll be in lockup over the weekend, at which time, on Monday, you'll be arraigned."

As we made a right turn onto South Racine Avenue, there was a gathering of four young men standing on the corner. They were laughing, slapping each other high fives. Then one of them put his middle finger up just as the SUV passed. I'd read an article not long ago about a woman who had flipped off the president's motorcade. So maybe this was a new trend.

I thought about my mama and how she would react to the news of my latest encounter with the government and with law enforcement. Mama, who of course was getting older, just wanted to live life now as a freedwoman. Not be locked away like a caged animal aching for another shot at freedom. I truly understood her thinking, but I knew that my life called for forging a different path.

When we arrived at the police station, the FBI agent in the passenger seat got out and opened the back door. He was talking on his cell phone to someone in a manner, which I did not understand. As if he were receiving detailed instructions about what to do with me. I wondered whom he could have been talking to. I wondered where I would ultimately find myself after this initial phase of my arrest.

I was escorted into the station and then almost immediately met with stares. It was a place I'd become intimately familiar with from the night of the Michigan Avenue protests when Marcus was tussled to the ground and ultimately arrested. And before that, the night of my graduation and commencement speech, when Federal agents chased me out of Soldier Field, leading me to eventually turn myself in.

I was led into an area where I was instructed to

stand against a cinder-block wall to have my picture taken. I had seen booking photos before on late-night TV. But it's a heck of a lot more humiliating when you're having a mug shot taken that anyone with a computer can see. I thought about all of my classmates from Chicago Prep Academy. I thought about the thousands of people who'd heard my speech as valedictorian, and who had possibly been following my journey. I also thought of all the teachers who had supported me and were certain that I would go on to do well in life. What would they think of me now?

Another officer came up to me as I moved away from the spot where arrestees are told to stand. He looked much older than the other cops here on duty. In fact, he looked like someone that should have already retired. He said nothing as I approached, only pointed to a machine. I moved closer to the front of it as he reached out for my hand. One by one he held each of my fingers, dabbed them in ink and rolled them across the flat of the glass. "It's not every day that someone is brought in accompanied by the FBI. Especially at your age," the cop mused.

I glanced up at him. "Well, I'm hoping that I won't be here long."

The officer smiled. "I sincerely doubt you'll be going anywhere soon. But there's nothing wrong with wishful thinking."

After he finished with my last finger, he grabbed a paper towel and handed it to me.

"I grew up in the 60s before you were born. I saw it all transpire in real time. The ugly violence of the Civil Rights Movement and the race riots. The assassinations of both Martin Luther King Jr. and JFK. And the Vietnam War," he said.

Despite this cop's effort to try and establish some common ground, I imagined it impossible for him to know what it felt like being a person of color. I imagined that word had gotten around quickly why I had been arrested. I'm sure that the presence of two FBI agents had had a lot to do with it. The officer put some things away and then began escorting me down a corridor. "So, what made you become a policeman?" I asked him.

Standing much taller, he glanced down. "There were several reasons. It was a family tradition for one. My grandfather and uncle were cops. Although more than anything—I wanted to help people who couldn't help themselves. But would I be a cop in today's climate if I were just starting out?" He shook his head. "I don't think so."

As we walked, the thought of being locked in a cell, even if only for a few days—until someone could possibly post bail—had become my stark new reality. I wondered what Mama would think. And what she'd say upon hearing about my latest run-in with the authorities. Suddenly on my left, I heard footsteps and a voice that sounded all too familiar. I looked up and saw that it was Ariel's father walking toward me as the cop held my arm.

"Ariel and Marcus weren't allowed in. Neither was anyone else. There's also a small crowd gathering outside. Are you okay?" he asked.

Before I could nod or even answer, the policemen interjected.

"And who are you?" The cop asked.

"I'm her dad. I have every right to be here. I'm waiting for our family attorney."

The officer looked at me, then at Ariel's father. "You don't say. Now that you mention it . . . I think I can see the resemblance." He shook his head. "No visitation until authorization is given." The cop pulled my arm and continued taking me through a long corridor. While trying to keep his pace, I managed to swivel my head and noticed Ariel's father charging toward the glass doors out onto Michigan Avenue.

Coming toward us on our left was another female in handcuffs. Her face was bleeding from a small cut beneath her right eye. And she was cursing apparently at no one in particular.

Minutes later I was led into a room that included a small round table and several chairs. There was a mirror on the wall. I'd watched enough late-night cop shows to know that it was probably a window to someone watching from the other side. I'm also sure that whatever I had to say would be recorded. "What is going on? What's going to happen to me?" I asked.

The cop pulled out a chair and motioned for me to sit. Then he walked over to a file cabinet and poured himself a glass of water. "Want some?"

I shook my head. "No."

"Before you're taken to your cell, the feds would like to talk to you. You must have really ruffled their feathers." He jerked his chin. "A young black girl like you? Not something we see too often."

I leaned forward and clasped my hands on the table. "The only thing I'm guilty of is trying to make a difference in the world. I'm sure you would agree that there's a lot of room for improvement?"

The officer nodded. "Yeah, there's a lot of room for improvement."

"Do you have any kids?" I asked matter-of-factly.

"Who me? Married and divorced twice. No kids. Actually, I'm thankful because the way this world has gotten, I could only imagine what it would be like for my grandchildren in the future. No thanks."

Three men walked into the room from the hallway. Two of them I recognized as the FBI agents from the church. The other I recognized as agent Haupht, whom Mama and I had sat with for hours regarding what the government wanted to know about our past. I remembered him as being the agent in charge, the one who'd made it clear that we were not to tell anyone about our secret.

He unbuttoned his coat and set what looked like a miniature tape recorder on the table. "Officer, we'll be taking over from here." I watched as the only man in uniform abruptly left the room. I wondered if my only chance at maintaining at least a small degree of anonymity had gone with him.

Agent Haupht sat and retrieved a folded piece of paper from his suit jacket. "On October 24th you organized, online, a boycott of three of the nation's largest food manufacturers. Four weeks later, on the day before Thanksgiving, you organized a protest downtown at Daley Plaza in which several Chicago police officers were injured." He glanced up at me. "Assaulted by several known and documented gang members."

"It was a demonstration," I corrected.

Agent Haupht leaned forward. His eyes bore into mine. "It doesn't matter what you or I choose to call it. The fact of the matter is that you are now identified as a Black Identity Extremist."

I wondered what that term meant exactly. Was it just a label to keep tabs on someone who'd fought racial injustice and sought equality? And how could it be any more of a threat than someone who had identified him or herself as a white supremacist?

Agent Haupht took a deep breath and leaned back in his chair. "You're a smart young woman. Brave. And you've already been given one hell of a second chance— the likes of which the world has never seen before. You're worth more to society on the outside compared to what little you could accomplish sitting inside of a jail cell. But not *this* way, not the way you're going about it. Quite frankly, Lula, you're skating on thin ice here."

"I just want to right what I see is wrong. I see this as the only way progress will be made."

"I understand that. However, there *is* a better

way to handle what it is you're trying to accomplish," Haupht said.

I shook my head and met his stare. "I guess we just see things differently."

"Be advised . . . there are a million different ways that we can deal with this situation, Lula. I don't think you want to push your luck. I want you to consider this your final warning."

The more I sat and listened the more I saw myself sinking deeper into a bottomless pit. I figured that I'd already said enough and that the more I continued to talk the deeper into the rabbit hole I'd go. "I have nothing else to say," I muttered. "I want to talk to a lawyer."

Agent Haupht clasped his hands on the table. "You won't be needing one. Because we're letting you go. We're authorizing your release tonight on the condition that you and your mother go about the rest of your lives as good law abiding citizens. You both are very fortunate. You have a lot to be thankful for. Don't mess this up!"

The FBI agent who had been standing by but never said a word went to open the door. Agent Haupht grabbed his coat, and then I saw him talking to several police officers including one who I assumed was a sergeant.

Suddenly a policeman, a brute of a man, came charging into the room. "Stand up and stick out your hands." He grabbed a small key from a metal ring and began removing my handcuffs. "You're free to go . . . for now. Let's hope you stay out of trouble."

I glanced up at him without saying a word. Then I walked through the corridor trying to find my way to the front of the building. Immediately I spotted Ariel's father pacing near the entrance, probably waiting for the family attorney. He turned just in time to see me walking toward him. He looked astounded at my presence. He grinned broadly. "They're letting you go? You're free to go home?"

I nodded. "Yes. I'll have to tell you all about it, everything the FBI said."

"Well, the last thing you need is a criminal record. You'll lose your job and any chance of remaining a teacher." Looking past his shoulder, I saw Marcus and Ariel outside talking to a group of people while holding signs. "What are they doing?" I asked.

He turned around. "Oh, they've organized an impromptu protest asking that you be released. Looks like it might have helped." He clapped a hand on my shoulder. "Come on, let's get you home." We walked out onto South Michigan Avenue and were instantly met with cheers from the small crowd that had gathered. "I knew they had no choice but to let you go!" Marcus exclaimed as both he and Ariel rushed over to hug me. Not far behind them was a contingent of reporters. But several policemen came outside to maintain some semblance of order and blocked them from getting closer.

I appreciated the support that Marcus and Ariel had always given me. But sometimes I wondered if they actually understood the real seriousness of what we were doing. Perhaps it was because we had come from two different places in human history, me as a slave—and them—born into absolute freedom.

Walking up the sidewalk and flanked by several beefy men who appeared to be his security was Father Bigos. Next to him and surrounded by several other men was Jay Killa.

"We postponed the meeting, and I wanted to get over here right away to see about your well being," Father Bigos murmured.

"Thank you. They've released me, but with a rather stern warning."

The Catholic priest pulled me into his embrace. "Don't let them discourage you from what you're doing, Lula. You're doing good work the way I see it." Then he stood back, his hands resting squarely on my shoulder as we met eye to eye. "You keep on keeping on," he said. "Keep fighting the good fight!"

I had seen Father Bigos on television many times speaking out against crime in the communities of people of color. But to actually be standing in front of police headquarters receiving his full-on support meant more to me than he could have ever known.

After several minutes of acknowledging the courageous efforts of the crowd who had braved dropping temperatures, I was carefully whisked into Ariel's father's car. Whatever my next move was going to be, whatever I had planned next, I was going to keep silent. For the last hour and a half, I had been resisting the need to go to the bathroom. Now it was time to go home—regroup—think things over. And spend the rest of the evening with Mama.

CHAPTER 6

PASTOR TOMPKINS CALLED me early on Saturday morning to remind me that I'd promised to fill in for him by visiting former convicts at a halfway house on the far West side. It was a privately funded residence called New Beginnings of Chicago Lawndale, a three-story greystone that had been converted to house recently released convicted felons. Its primary purpose, he told me, was to assist them in getting on their feet and to hopefully turn their lives around by making positive contributions to society.

When he had called earlier in the week, Pastor Tompkins had told me that he could not make it because he was scheduled to give the Eulogy at a funeral for one of the long-time deacons of his church. He'd also mentioned that the halfway house had been in danger of closing unless a grant from some generous, anonymous donor could come through in a Hail Mary at the last minute to save it. Apparently, it must have been important to show whomever this person was that there were still people who cared about giving these men a second chance.

I rummaged through my closet looking for something casual and conservative to wear. But the only things I found that didn't need washing or taken to the cleaners were a pair of Levis and a blouse that I'd bought at Akira on a shopping trip with Ariel. After putting on my clothes, I quickly pulled my hair into a knot and headed out the door.

To my surprise, Mama had wanted to accompany me this morning. Maybe because she had been concerned about my safety. Or perhaps she was concerned that I'd somehow be arrested again. Or maybe my mother felt like this was a trip she needed to make to offer some sliver of hope to formerly wayward men of color. After leaving our apartment, we stopped at a McDonald's drive-thru. Mama ordered a McCafé Coffee and breakfast burrito while I ordered a Sausage McMuffin with Egg.

"How much do you *really* know about Pastor Tompkins?" Mama asked.

I turned to look at her as the drive-thru cashier handed me our bag. "What do you mean?"

"I'm just concerned about you, baby girl. I don't mean you no harm, and don't wanna interfere with your purpose in life. But sometimes . . . I think you can be too trusting of people. After all, he *does* have a checkered past. Tried to take some money that didn't belong to him. *And that's a fact!*"

I couldn't believe what I was hearing. I pulled out of the McDonald's parking lot and immediately turned into the rotted driveway of an old tire repair shop. I quickly switched off my car's engine. "Mama. You're suspicious of Pastor Tompkins? Why?"

Mama lifted up in her seat and turned toward me. "A leopard never changes its spots." She shook her head. "You and I are still getting used to this bold new world and the times we are living in, Lula. It's different now. Back then, we knew who to watch out for. And with the kind of work you're doing you've got to know exactly who to trust. That's all I'm trying to say."

'I just believe that anyone who's made mistakes in the past can turn their life around. That's one of the reasons why I've volunteered to go to the West Side this morning. Now until Pastor Tompkins proves otherwise, I feel confident I'm doing the right thing by giving him the benefit of the doubt."

I started the car, pulled out of the driveway, and then merged into traffic. Mama turned away, focusing on the scenery out the window. I imagined she thought that I was being stubborn, and would have to learn things the hard way. That I would be the only one between us to have graduated with honors from the School of Hard Knocks. I turned on the radio to *The Vick and Tammy Morning Show*, where, ironically, "A Change is Gonna Come" by Sam Cooke was playing.

Eventually, we'd made it to the West Side and parked directly in front of the building. Coming down the sidewalk was a young woman carrying a baby. When we made eye contact with her, she crossed the street. Mama and I walked inside and stood in front of a mahogany desk that sat in the middle of what would normally be considered a living room. Then, out of a nearby space appeared a short and stocky woman carrying a large cardboard box.

"I take it you all are here in place of my good friend, Pastor Tompkins, is that correct?"

I nodded. "Yes, ma'am. Lula and Ella Mae Darling. How did you know?"

"He told me you'd be filling in for him. Marquita Robinson-Jackson, I'm the director here," she said offering her hand. "The pastor lends himself whenever he has some free time. Which is about once a month as his schedule permits. Follow me." Marquita spun on her heels and began walking down a dark blue carpeted hallway. "We're all about impacting lives, inspiring positive change," she muttered as she gasped for breath. Then she opened a closet and sat the box down on the floor. "These young men really need it. Pastor Tompkins is a mentor to them. Probably the only positive male figure many of them have ever had in life."

After she closed the door, we followed Marquita toward the back of the building up a flight of stairs. Immediately I reached out to the wall on my right, and the railing on our left because the steps felt spongy and uneven. Marquita glanced at us. "I want you to meet Darius. Out on parole for a drug offense. He was selling heroin and got busted during an undercover sting operation. He's the one that Reverend Tompkins has been spending the most time with." She stopped abruptly in the second floor's darkened hallway and then turned toward

Mama and me. "Before we go into his room, gracing him with our presence, I need to give you both a heads up. Darius can be very hot-tempered whenever feeling either threatened or challenged. He grew up in a foster home not far from here. He never knew his biological parents. Bottom line is he feels like he doesn't quite fit in the world—like society owes him something for his pain."

Mama and I exchanged glances. I wondered if it had been a good idea by bringing her with me. The door to the young man's room was partially open. But Marquita had gently knocked anyway. "Darius, I have some people I'd like for you to meet."

"I don't feel like meeting nobody."

Marquita pushed the door open further. "They're here in place of Pastor Tompkins. They know him. He sent them over because he couldn't make it out today." Darius was lying in bed eating a bowl of cereal, watching a football game on television. He looked twenty-something and was wearing a blue sweatshirt and a pair of jeans. A black doo-rag tightly gripped his head.

"I have to go see about the others. I'll let the three of you be so that you all can get acquainted." Marquita turned and walked out of the room. I could hear the floor creak as she sauntered down the hallway and then down the stairs.

Darius sat up straight on the bed. "You all got some money for me? You going to tell me I don't have to stay here no more?"

He sat his bowl of cereal on top of a black milk crate, then rose to his feet and began walking toward Mama and me. "Because if you don't . . . we might have a problem up in this place!"

Mama and I exchanged a nervous glance. Then Mama gently let her purse slide off her shoulder into her hand. I imagined what she had planned to do with it if Darius took one step closer. "We're only here to offer some moral support, some guidance. Nothing more," Mama murmured.

"Moral support? I look like I need moral support to you?"

He shifted his gaze from my mother's to mine. "I . . . I um." I searched for words that would not come for fear that I would say the wrong thing. Darius's eyes went wide as he waited for a response. Then he burst out laughing. "I'm just messing with y'all. It's been a long time since I seen somebody look *that* scared. Y'all can't be scared like that coming 'round here."

He turned to lower the volume on the television, and then grabbed his breakfast and went to the window, staring out of it. "But for real, though, I got to get back on my feet. Get out there and make me some money."

"And how exactly do you plan to do that?" I asked him. "Sell drugs?"

He turned around. "You didn't hear me say that now did you? If it hadn't been for that old dude filming us from his second-floor living room window —I wouldn't be standing here talkin' to you right now! The public defender told us that he had *hours* of footage of us on the corner. That old fool was even recording it when they arrested us! Had the nerve to come out onto his porch in his robe. Taunting my homie and me as they placed us in the back of the police car, he said, *It done finally caught up with you. I was taping you punks the whole time, poisoning your own people with that hair-on you putting in them plastic bags. I don't feel sorry for you losers.* I shook my head and looked over at the dude I was with, OG 12X, twelve meaning the number of times he's shot someone. Man, he went completely ballistic! It took four cops just to hold him back. Meanwhile, the police slammed the door, and I looked out the window. I could still hear the old man going in on us. As the car started to move, he came down the steps of the porch and yelled, *I don't feel no empathy for you! You done got what you deserved! Dat's rite!*

Darius lifted his bowl and scooped up a spoonful of cereal. "I guess he didn't see all the White folks who were coming to the hood from the suburbs to get their fix. I was told that he doesn't live there anymore. Trust me when I tell you . . . I still have *nightmares* hearing that old, scruffy voice of his shouting that stuff from across the street!"

Listening to Darius talk, I imagined that he, like a lot of today's youth, was full of potential. But somehow had the misfortune of being misguided along their life's path, or perhaps had fell victim of having no guidance at all. It was like they were still enslaved to a way of thinking that was contrary to them living up to their full potential. Darius, I hoped, still had a lot of life ahead of him. Although the real question was . . . what he'd planned to do with it.

"You seem like an intelligent guy, Darius. You ever asked yourself how did you end up here, meaning at this point in your life?" I asked him.

Darius sat on the edge of his bed. He shrugged. "I grew up in a foster home. My mother gave me up for adoption when I was born. I never knew who my father was. The coward skipped out before I had even entered the world, I was told. The foster lady who raised me, Ms. Butler, she died when I was sixteen."

Immediately my eyes were drawn to an old color photo Darius had pinned above his bed. "Is that her? Is that Ms. Butler?" I asked.

"Yeah. That was her when she first moved to Chicago from Louisiana. She passed away about five years later. After that, I was pretty much raised on the streets. And if you know anything about *these* streets, you know to either dog, or you *get* dogged."

"There's a whole other world out there," I corrected. "There are different paths, different opportunities available to you if you would be open to seeking them. If you go back to doing what you were doing before, you're either going to find yourself back in jail—or perhaps—dead."

Darius glanced up at me. "So, what do I do?"

"I've started a Movement to help right the wrongs that I see in the world. And from being here talking to you today, I believe that you could be instrumental in what I am doing. I believe that we can help each other, Darius. Are you willing to give it a try?"

"Yeah, I am. Because my homies are getting shot up out here in these streets. And because *I will die before I have to go back to jail.* Y'all don't have a clue what it's like to be stuck in a cell, to not have your freedom for a long period of time."

I looked at Mama, back at Darius, and then nodded. "Actually . . . I think we do." I opened my purse and pulled out a pamphlet that outlined the Movement's objectives, dates and times of future meetings. "Here's some information about what I'm doing. Why don't you come to our next gathering with an open mind and a changed heart to find out more about what we have planned? My contact info is at the bottom."

I reached out my hand to give Darius the material as he rose from the bed. "All right, I'll be there. I guess there's no harm in checking it out, I suppose. Hopefully, you can find me a job, so I don't have to go back to hustling!"

Later that evening Mama and I returned home to get any signs of stress off our minds completely. She went into her bedroom to watch reruns of *Grey's Anatomy*. I went directly to my laptop to check my emails. Immediately I noticed an urgent message from Father Bigos. I clicked to open it. He wanted to let me know that one of the biggest electronics manufacturers in the world, after unrelenting pressure, had agreed to build their new headquarters on the outskirts of downtown Chicago. This was a huge and major win for not only the Movement but more importantly, for the people of Chicago. The young. The disenfranchised. This would mean thousands of new jobs, new opportunities to pick up a skill instead of a felony, to provide for their families.

I could not have been more pleased with the results that our efforts had gotten. I looked at this as a potential blueprint that could be applied in other major cities.

Immediately I closed my laptop and bolted into Mama's room to give her the good news. But as soon as I had made it through the door, I saw that she was lying on her side off into a deep sleep. I thought of how there was a time when she didn't have the luxury of sleeping on a bed of her own, surrounded by the comfort of privacy. After toting her around Lawndale, and with Sunday morning service merely hours away, the last thing I wanted to do was wake her.

CHAPTER 7

MARCUS INVITED ARIEL, Tommy and I to a video shoot of his new song, "Unfaithful" which had been co-produced by Jay Killa. Ariel's parents had decided to hold off on celebrating their twenty-fifth wedding anniversary, a weekend trip to Lake Geneva, Wisconsin and had agreed to watch Thomas Jr. instead. The four of us drove to an abandoned warehouse, which stood as the back-drop. I had also invited me and Mama's cousin, JuJu, whom we'd met on a trip to Gary, Indiana when we went to learn if we'd had any living kin. JuJu was an up and coming wannabe rapper, so he was more than delighted to be a part of the shoot.

When we arrived, there was a row of white video production vans parked along the curb. One of them had been equipped with a mobile studio,

Marcus told us, so that in the event inspiration struck, he and Jay Killa could lay down new music at their own discretion. When we exited Marcus's SUV, almost immediately Jay Killa came walking over to the parking lot to say hello.

He smiled as he removed his trademark sunglasses. "I see you all have arrived fabulously late. It's all good, though. Cray Williams, the director, is still working on some technical issues with the cameramen. Nevertheless, we should begin shooting very soon. So how are you feeling this morning, Marcus? You good?"

Marcus nodded. "Yeah, I'm good. I can't complain. Because my girl, Lula, is doing her thing, slowly changing lives for the better. And because I got a feeling *this* song is gonna blow straight up! I can feel it, Jay. Besides, my girl and my best friends came down here this morning just to support me."

"Well, that's good stuff. Everyone needs a support system. Especially in this business. If you don't watch it, you can lose yourself." Jay Killa turned around and summoned a young biracial-looking woman to come toward us. "Speaking of support I want the rest of you to meet, Nikkida, she's playing me and Marcus's love interest in the video. And in case he didn't tell you, we're both unknowingly competing for her affection in it. She's an Instagram model. Cray discovered her, and then reached out to her to see if she was interested."

Nikkida had barely anything covering her chest, even despite the cold weather. As she walked over, JuJu's eyes grew wide, pinning her with his gaze. He was the first one to step forward, extending his hand. "There's also security at both ends of the street. Some off-duty police officers. Because as each of you very well knows, filming a music video like we're doing can attract the wrong element," Killa went on.

Several minutes later, our attention was drawn to two cameramen who had been standing on the sidewalk. Apparently, the director was having a heated discussion with one of the employees of Killa's record label. We followed Jay Killa and Marcus as they went to prevent what looked like was going to be a nuclear meltdown. There had been rumors on the street that Jay Killa had become increasingly frustrated with his record label. He had even planted an idea in Marcus's head that the two of them could form their own independent record company and partner with a major label for distribution.

As we got closer, a large middle-aged man was

pointing down at a camera in his left hand. There were a few moments of silence. Then Cray turned toward Killa shaking his head. "I'm sorry, Jay. But we're gonna have to reschedule. We're having some technical issues that we'll need to address. I'm just as disappointed as you are. I know that you and Marcus want to get this right!"

Killa shook his head. "Dude, couldn't this have been prevented? Each time we come out, it costs us money. *Serious money*. And each and every cent . . . me and Marcus have to pay for with our future royalties."

The few times I've been around him, I'd never seen Jay Killa this upset. I looked down both ends of the block and saw several men coming toward us. I assumed that they were the off-duty cops that Killa had been referring to. Immediately I nudged an elbow at Marcus. "It's best that we reschedule like they're suggesting. Maybe something can be worked out with the record company," I said.

Marcus agreed and then clapped a hand on his mentor's shoulder. "Look, don't sweat it, Jay. Things happen, and this is totally beyond our control. We'll just reschedule. Maybe even come up with some better ideas for the next shoot. Everything happens for a reason."

"As long as you're okay with it," Killa said.

Marcus nodded "Yeah, I'm okay with it. I mean, do we really have a choice?" He and Killa embraced as the entire production crew packed up their equipment and prepared to leave. Then Killa walked to the parking lot and got into a black Escalade.

"Well, I haven't had breakfast yet. And I'm assuming that the rest of you haven't either. There's a place over on Washington Boulevard. Both their omelets and cheese grits are on point. Don't worry about the cost. It's all on me. I'm paying for every-body!" Marcus announced.

The six of us, including Nikkida, trailed each other in our cars to the restaurant. The place was spacious with a Southern-inspired menu, juice bar and was conveniently located in the West Loop. After a several minute wait, we were seated at a large table. Nikkida took out her compact mirror to check her makeup and swiped some hair away from her eye. "So, I want to thank you and Jay for the opportunity to be in your video, Marcus." She smiled. "It means a lot for a wannabe actress like myself to get some exposure."

Marcus nodded as he sipped a glass of fresh squeezed orange juice. "Glad to be in a position to help. Believe me, I know how rough it is trying to get noticed when you don't know anyone. Jay told me you've recently relocated here. How did you end up in Chicago?" he asked.

"Trust me when I tell you, I've been everywhere else, and the competition for acting gigs is cutthroat. I know they're starting to film more and more here. You know, shows like *Empire?* So I'm here just looking for my big break. I could also tell you about some of the nightmares I've had to live through. But I don't think you're ready to hear about my life as a video vixen."

Tommy laughed. "Now you've got our interest piqued." He shook his head. "Don't bring it up if you're not going to spill the beans. Or maybe you're waiting to eventually write a tell-all book."

"What? No, nothing like that. But this industry —it can be really creepy. I grew up in LA and also spent some time in New York. I remember this one time . . . there was this producer who had invited me to his house to see some of his work. When I arrived, he came to the door with nothing but a robe on. So I thought, okay, maybe he was behind schedule and wasn't ready in time for our meeting. Being young, naïve, and chasing a dream of fame and fortune had clearly clouded my judgment. At first, he took me on a tour of his massive home. I thought it strange that I didn't see anyone else. No wife. No kids. Not even a maid or housekeeper. Then he led me into a large room. The first thing I noticed was the silver projector hanging from the ceiling, rows of reclining leather seats, a huge black curtain. He called it his screening room." Nikkida drew in a deep breath. "We sat and watched a montage of his entertainment industry credits, his awards, and accomplishments. Then he showed me some videos of two female singing groups. He claimed to have been responsible for their success. For getting several of their songs included on a major motion picture soundtrack. I must admit that I was very impressed. As I watched the last video come to an end, as the curtains in front of the screen closed, I was more than eager to get started on my own career as an actress. Then things went completely south."

Marcus furrowed his brow. "What happened?"

"He stood up right next to me, and then he disrobed. He had absolutely nothing on underneath. He simply stared at me, and then said: *You have to give up something if you expect to get what you want. That's how this works. That's how most deals get made.* Then he positioned himself over me as I sat in the chair. I was confused, nervous, frozen. 'This was not what I was expecting,' I told him. 'This is not what I want!' He became angry very quickly. He moved forward to get on top of me. I managed to push him off using my arms, hands, and feet. Then I bolted for the front entrance and ran outside to my car."

Marcus shook his head and pointed. "You, are a brave woman. Did you call the police?"

Nikkida leaned back in her chair and folded her arms. "Honestly, no. I did not. But I should have. I think there was a part of me that wondered if anyone would believe me. Here I was . . . a young woman, barely legal—making an accusation against a well-known and powerful man. I'm thankful I don't have to worry about that with you and your label, Marcus." Nikkida dropped her arms to her side and leaned forward. I imagined that she was ready to take the attention off of her and divert it to someone, or something else. I imagined that she had had a brief moment to consider, that she had talked more than she had wanted. "Speaking of being a brave woman . . . Lula, I heard through the grapevine that you're somewhat of a community activist. Is that true?"

I was right. I nodded. "I am. I consider it to be my calling. My life's purpose."

Nikkida raised her hand for a fist bump. "Well, my hat's off to you, girl. You *have* to be brave to do something like that. To stand up for what is right by yourself like that. All I can say is . . . just watch yourself."

I knew very well the dangers of what I was doing, but I was curious to hear Nikkida's take on why she thought what I was doing was so dangerous. "What makes you say that?"

"Girl, ain't nobody trying to see poor folks out here get ahead. Especially poor people of color. And then, some of us even act like we don't *want* any help. Like we've accepted our current condition in this country as our permanent reality."

I stared at Nikkida as she said this. It was clearly apparent to me that one of her parents could have actually been white. But she seemed to have identified more with her black side. I imagined that when it was time to check the box for race or ethnic background on a job application or census, her choice would undoubtedly be to identify as black or African-American. "We have to hate racism and injustice more than we hate ourselves," I corrected. "We have plenty of money to spend but are not spending it wisely, in my opinion. Not in a way where it would benefit us and our community."

Nikkida glanced over at Ariel and Tommy. She probably wondered if they had felt uncomfortable because they were white having to sit in on a conversation about the empowerment of people of color. About downplaying their white privilege to appear, they could relate to our struggle.

Our food had finally arrived. And most of the conversation had taken a back seat to us feeding our appetite. JuJu, who had been quiet the whole time we were here, pulled out his cell phone while looking at the screen. It was obvious he was reading a text. "Okay, before I forget, my uncle, Joe Gatlin, said that you are all cordially invited to a family get together we're having next weekend. It's going to be at a banquet hall in our hometown of Gary, Indiana. It's also his seventy-fifth birthday. I'll group text the time and address. And Lula, he said that you can bring whomever you want. But to make sure you bring your mother, Ella Mae."

CHAPTER 8

ON THE DAY of the Gatlin family gathering and Joe Gatlin's birthday, Mama was in as good a mood as I'd ever seen her. For forty-five minutes she had been holed up in her room crooning her favorite songs. Everything from old Negro spirituals to "How I Got Over" by Mahalia Jackson. For several seconds I peeked through the doorway and saw my mother standing in front of the mirror. She studied herself in 360-degree fashion while wearing a gray pantsuit, an outfit she had purchased on clearance at T.J.Maxx.

At 5 p.m. we got in my car, proceeded Southbound on Stony Island Avenue, connected to I-80, and then headed East to Cline Avenue in Gary. When we arrived, I had immediately noticed: *Congratulations Joe* in black letters on the white sign outside of the building. We must have gotten there before anyone else because the parking lot was almost entirely empty. Since cousin Joe had given me the green light to bring whomever I wanted, I'd also invited Marcus and Mama D., Ariel and Tommy, and Pastor Tompkins and whomever he wanted to bring as his date. Whether they would all show up or not was anyone's guess.

When Mama and I entered, we had no idea where to go. To our right, down a hall, there was some loud noise, like the clanking sound of some heavy equipment. We followed the noise and came to a room where a DJ was in a corner setting up his stuff. The room was filled with round, white linen-clothed tables. White and gold balloons hung from the ceiling. White balloons with the number 75 in gold. The gold balloons were embellished with Joe's name in white.

As soon as Mama and I sat down, we heard the sound of heels stride across the laminate wood floor. We both turned around to see who was approaching. "Good evening Ella Mae, Lula. Glad you could make it to help me celebrate my 75th birthday."

Joe was dressed fabulously in a black tuxedo, a crisp white shirt, shined patent leather shoes and a neat bow tie. His niece, Shantay, who was also me and Mama's cousin, was pushing him in his wheel-chair. We stood up and gave them both a hug. "Now Joe, you *know* we wouldn't miss this special occasion," Mama mused. "How you feeling these days? You look well."

Joe met Mama's gaze. "Well as can be expected. You know I got my hands full with the peanut gallery. That's what I call my nieces and nephews. They take dysfunction to a whole new level." Joe smiled. "But I wouldn't have it any other way. I love 'em to death."

I thought how admirable it was that my cousin, now a senior citizen, had been caring for his sister's kids after her untimely death years ago. It was the really honorable thing to do, especially at a time in history where people didn't seem to care for each other like they once did.

The DJ pressed a button on the keyboard of his laptop and started playing "Ain't Too Proud To Beg," by the Temptations over a pair of JBL speakers. Joe was still talking, but now we were struggling to hear him. So Mama and I leaned over, offering our ears even closer. "I've got a photographer coming to get some good pictures of us. We've got some hot food being catered in by one of our relatives. And my longtime good friend, Stevie, will be here all the way from The Motor City—Detroit. He drove up by himself last night," he said smiling.

"A seventy-fifth birthday is an important milestone. It sounds like you have everything the way you want it," I replied. More of Joe's guests started to come inside. There were couples dressed in two-piece matching outfits. A small group of kids came in milling about. Several pairs of women, all apparently without a date. Then, Pastor Tompkins came walking in proudly with the woman he had introduced us to previously, his girlfriend, LaShonda Bishop.

Shantay's brothers arrived at several minutes after six, including JuJu, who, to my surprise, had Nikkida from the video shoot flanking his side as his date. Shantay went to the DJ's table and scooped up a microphone. Then she came toward us and handed it to Joe. He held the cordless mike as he looked across the room, squinting to see beneath the fluorescent lights.

"Thank you to everyone for coming out to help an old man celebrate. I want you all to know how much I appreciate it." He looked around. "So, that being said, everybody, please get acquainted. Have a good time. Take plenty of pictures that I can treasure for years to come. And last but not least, don't

THE RISE OF LULA DARLING

let this wheelchair fool you because I can still shake a leg. I might have to before this night is over. It may only be for a few seconds. But by the Grace of God, it's more than I could do a year ago."

There was a lot of cheering and catcalls. The banquet hall was near full capacity. I imagined that the owners had to have been making good money by the looks of how many other names were on the parking lot's sign tonight. I also wondered exactly who had owned it. I looked toward the entrance of the room and saw the caterer moving his steel cart to one side. Suddenly, coming in gingerly, and leaning heavily on her cane was Mama D., with Marcus holding her left elbow.

After dinner, Joe's best friend, Stevie, walked over to the DJ's table and recited a poem he had made in honor of he and Joe's sixty-year friendship. "I said that I wasn't gonna stand here and get all choked up." He pointed. "But that man right there is like a brother to me. There for me, and I hate to say this . . . but he's been there for me during tough times, more than members of my own family." He raised a glass of champagne in the air. "Love you, Joe. Happy 75th birthday, my friend."

Joe nodded in appreciation. "Thank you. Love you as well my brother." He cleared his throat.

"Now that everyone has eaten, I know you young people, and even some of you old ones are anxious to hit the dance floor. So Mr. DJ, it's time to cut it lose!"

I sat between Mama and Marcus finishing the last of a generous serving of apple pie a' la mode. Then I heard what sounded like a catfight brewing on our left. A woman in a red mini club dress, heels, wearing hoop earrings, pointed her finger across the table. The two of them seemed to be locked in a battle for who could talk more loudly than the other. At first, I thought it was a merely playful conversation. But then one of them lobbed a half-full glass of Moet & Chandon in the other's face. At that point, I knew things had gotten really serious.

Mama stood up and walked over to tell Joe about the disturbance. He was busy locked in conversation with an older friend, whom he'd intro-duced earlier as one of his running buddies during the time Joe owned his bar in Indiana. But Mama politely interjected, leaned over to whisper in our cousin's ear. "Excuse me," he said. Joe wheeled his wheelchair around and moved to the direction of the DJ's booth. The DJ had been crouched down behind a table pulling some cables from a cardboard box. He was also wearing a pair of black *Beats* headphones.

Marcus and I walked over to the table where the women sat, in an attempt to intervene. It was beginning to look more like a scene from one of those reality housewives shows than the festive atmosphere of a seventy-five-year-old's birthday party. As we approached the table, I quickly reached out to block a punch thrown by the woman in the red dress. I almost fell over the table trying to push her arm to the side.

Joe had finally gotten the DJ's attention, and he abruptly stopped the music. "Hold up. You both are totally out of line!" Mama D. shouted from the middle of the room. She struggled to get to her feet. JuJu came over from where he had been sitting to help her stand. He escorted Mama D. over to the left side of the room as Marcus and I tried our best to keep these two female gladiators from killing each other.

Mama D. pointed. "What's your name?"

"Vanessa."

"And what's yours?"

"Angelique."

Mama D. looked at both women, her faced

pained with grief. "What could you have possibly been fighting over to have made such a scene?"

"She needs to understand that my man is off limits. I don't share him with nobody!" said Vanessa.

"If he's *your* man . . . then why is he texting and calling me all times of the night? And throughout the day. I'm jus sayin' " Angelique snapped.

Mama D. held out her arm over the table. "You two are *not* going to do this here. You're *not* going to ruin this nice man's celebration. *There are children here!* Now I would normally ask that you both be immediately shown the door. But I'm not going to do that. You're both going to listen to what this old woman has to say." Mama D. turned around. "Will someone bring over a microphone, please?"

JuJu walked to the DJ's table and brought the cordless mike over and handed it to Mama D.

"Is this thing on?" she asked, turning and gripping it with her hand. Suddenly there was a loud squeal of feedback.

"Hold it away from the speakers," the DJ said.

"Where is he?" Mama D. asked.

"Who?"

"Your boyfriend, or whatever you call him."

"He couldn't make it. He had another obligation," Vanessa hissed.

Mama D. shook her head. "Another obligation. And you don't know what that *is*, do you? For all you both know he could be with girlfriend number three." Both of these women stared at Marcus's grandmother as if she had lost her mind.

Mama D. hunched over and plopped her elbows on the table as her cane clattered to the floor. "Now, I'm probably older than anybody in here tonight. So I think that gives me an inalienable right to speak on the concept of living, and on some of life's most basic experiences." Mama D. switched back and forth, pinning each woman with her gaze. She followed with a stern look. "The first thing I'm going to say to both of you ladies is that if he's splitting his time between the two of you? Then he doesn't belong to either one of you in the first place, okay?" She drew in a deep breath. "Second, there's an old saying that the same way you got him, is the same way you will lose him. Bottom line is . . . if you're looking for loyalty from a man, then you both need to look elsewhere! *'Cause that man gonna have y'all crazy as a bat in a henhouse!*"

Mama D. straightened up as JuJu handed her her cane. She looked across the room. I admired her courageousness and her willingness to say something when others were often afraid to. Especially at the stage in life when most seniors her age would rather avoid conflict. Would rather live as far from the edge as humanly possible.

"Now, everyone here in this hall, as far as I'm concerned, is like family. Like the extended branches of a large tree. The problem is many of you young people today have lost your way. You've let that idiot box, what I call television, make you act like complete and utter damn fools. Influencing you to turn on one another, to turn away from what is *good*, what is *right*, *to turn away from God*. Someone needs to tell the truth without worry about sounding politically correct. I've lived a long time, and I see where this thing is going."

Mama D. turned. "And to be honest with you—in case you haven't noticed—where we're headed is not good. *Not good at all!* The choice is up to each and every one of us to do the right thing. Because I guarantee you, if we live according to the way He wants us to, we'll have a much better outcome," she said as she pointed to the ceiling. "Just give it a try and see if I'm lying to you. Now let's respect each other, here tonight, and going forward. Let's allow Mr. Gatlin to have his night without any problems. And let's enjoy ourselves in a *dignified* manner."

Vanessa shifted, batted her eyelids, then reached across the table to shake Angelique's hand. "Sorry, girlfriend. You know how it is when you love—"

"Love to a fault, I know. No need to explain, apology accepted," Angelique said.

Mama D. handed the microphone back to JuJu. And Marcus and I escorted her back to our table. The DJ turned up the volume slowly, playing a song that was more appropriate for the moment: "Smooth Sailing" by the Isley Brothers.

Joe wheeled himself back to our table. "Thank you all for intervening. I guess it wouldn't be a Gatlin family get together without some type of drama."

Mama D. leaned over. "Mr. Gatlin, I sure am glad to meet your acquaintance. I know we've never met personally, but through the good things I've heard about you, well, I feel a kindred spirit in common. Delores Whitaker," she said, extending her hand.

"I'm just thankful things did not get any worse. Thankful that that woman over there didn't pull out a gun or whatnot. Anyone who watches the news these days can see very clearly, that folks no longer value life anymore. It's really a shame." Joe panned his gaze among the four of us. "But enough of this doom and gloom talk. I want you all to enjoy the rest of my party. Because that's exactly what I intend to do!" He smiled and spun around in his wheelchair. I watched as he rolled out to the middle of the dance floor. Shantay joined him, her dancing in front of him as he beamed and clapped, contentedly.

Several minutes later Pastor Tompkins and his date walked over. "Good to be among you this evening, family." He furrowed his brow and smiled. "Delores, every time I think I've seen you at your best, you seem to surprise me one more time."

Mama D. nodded in appreciation. "Well, pastor, as you very well know, sometimes we're called in moments that will test our character."

"Yes, we are." Pastor Tompkins turned toward me. "And Lula, I can't say I was surprised to see you spring into action."

"I just did what I thought needed to be done. I really tried to prevent things from escalating."

"You did the right thing." Pastor Tompkins smiled again and put an arm around his date's shoulders. "Well, we're heading back early this evening. I've still got to prepare for service in the morning. Can we expect the four of you there, or will you be sleeping in after partying all night?"

"You can count me in, Pastor," my mother announced, raising her hand.

Mama D. glanced up. "I plan on being there too. Now, if I can get Marcus up and about early enough, and Lula to join him, I'll be tickled pink."

"Well, I hope to see you there." Pastor Tompkins turned and waved as he escorted his girlfriend toward the room's exit. "Good night, everybody."

As I watched he and his date walk out the door, I thought about what Mama D. had said about moments in which our character is tested. I thought about what could have happened if the woman whose arm I'd pushed away, had pulled out a gun or a knife. I thought about something I'd once heard somebody say: That life or death rests ultimately in the hands of God.

I know that there will be times when I'll face more disturbing moments than what occurred here tonight. Perhaps even more harrowing than my time spent in the previous century.

Suddenly Marcus grabbed my hand, jerking me out of my thoughts. "Come on . . . dance with me." He pulled me to my feet, and I followed him. We joined most of the guests on the floor with Joe

Gatlin in the middle, swaying in his wheelchair as the primary focus of attention. I looked his way and had to beam with joy and satisfaction. Because for this one moment in time, regardless of what had happened earlier, we were now enjoying each other's presence as one extended branch on the tree of human consciousness. As Mama D. had so eloquently put it when she spoke her usual pearls of wisdom…

We were all family.

CHAPTER 9

THE MOVEMENT WAS BEGINNING to take on a life of its own. My name was being increasingly tossed around in political circles. And local politicians had been attaching themselves to The Cause—and to me personally, whenever it meant them possibly securing extra votes. It was mostly done at election time and right before it was time to hit the campaign trail. Word had even spread internationally over social media about what I was doing, how I was now being referred to as a modern-day catalyst for change. Two weeks ago I had received an email from a young girl in Johannesburg, South Africa, informing me that I was her hero. How I had inspired her and others like her to help empower women in her country.

I imagined that the powers to be had also been

taking notice. Not just the local authorities, but also, the ones that are responsible for creating policy from afar, the movers and shakers that no one ever sees. Mama and I had been through a whirlwind of emotions. But now, I understood that everything we'd experienced had prepared us for what we would face going forward. I also understood that everything that had happened could work for our good if we allowed it to.

Marcus and Ariel had suggested that I take a break as a way to unwind from the mounting pressure and stress that I'd found myself under. We had all agreed to meet, relax, and to take our minds off our challenges for at least one day out of our busy lives. So I sat on Mama D.'s couch listening as Ariel and Tommy talked about where they would go on vacation once the weather turned. Several minutes later, Marcus had returned from running out to pick up a pizza. Mama D. was in her room lying in bed binge watching recorded episodes of *Family Feud*.

Marcus walked into the living room, set the pizza on top of a dinner tray. He took off his leather jacket and began to hand out paper plates. "I got a family size, half pepperoni, and half sausage, with a large order of buffalo wings." He grabbed the TV's remote from a small round wooden table and started flipping through channels. "Just as I suspected, there ain't nothing worth watching on television." He knelt down under the mantle and started rummaging through some albums inside of a milk crate.

"Marcus, what are you doing?" I asked him.

"I'm gonna play y'all some music. Mama D. gave me her Technics turntable when I graduated from high school. It still works like new; it still plays records. But you young folks wouldn't know nothing about that." Marcus turned toward the three of us sitting on the sofa. He started talking as if holding an imaginary microphone like he was an emcee about to address a restless audience. He smiled and suddenly went into full-on entertainment mode. "Don't you all worry. I won't subject you to listening to any of my own music today. Instead, I'm going to take you back in time. Back to a time when music spoke to the mind and to the heart. A time when music spoke to the *consciousness* of America. A time when music *meant* something by bringing forth social messages to the people."

"Yeah, speak on it, bro," Tommy mused as he chomped on a mouth full of food.

"You're referring to the sixties? What do you know about the time, Marcus?" I asked, smiling. We had agreed that the four of us would not talk business today. But Marcus had apparently wanted to open Pandora's Box. So I wanted to test his knowledge of the time in history when black folks were finally granted certain rights in America, the time before he had entered the world.

"Ladies and gentlemen, please observe in my hand, if you will, exhibit A. The album is appropriately entitled: 'We're A Winner' by the Impressions, including the late, great, Curtis Mayfield on vocals." Marcus set the twelve-inch on top of the record player and lowered the needle. "The name of this particular song is *also* called 'We're A Winner.' " He glanced up. "And I want to dedicate it to you, Lula, to all of us, and to anyone else who's involved in the struggle."

The music played, and as I listened to the lyrics, I was amazed at how much they seemed as relevant today as they did when first recorded. Marcus strolled over and reached out his hand asking me to dance with him. I got to my feet, and so did Ariel and Tommy.

"Excellent choice," I said as Marcus spun me around in front of him. He smiled and pulled me into his embrace. When the song was over, we sat down once again on the couch, finishing off the last of the pizza. Marcus rose and then pulled another album from the crate. "Now *this* one is from the Godfather of Soul himself, Mr. James Brown. It's called "I Don't Want Nobody to Give Me Nothing (Open Up the Door, I'll Get It Myself)." He set the needle onto the record and then slowly lowered the volume.

Ariel nodded as Marcus came over, sat on the sofa and grabbed a chicken wing. "How did you come across all this music and these records that were put out before you were born? They belong to Mama D?" she asked.

Marcus shook his head. "Actually, they belonged to my father. For the short time he was around, they're the only memories I have of him. I remember being barely able to stand while holding onto his leg as he played music in our living room. I remember him saying these were the songs he grew up listening to when *he* was a kid. So how did I get them? They were given to me when my mother lost her apartment, right after she got hooked on drugs."

I found myself thinking of what would happen to Marcus if suddenly Mama D. were no longer with us. I thought of how blessed he was to have a grandmother that stepped in to raise him.

"Just curious to know what's going on with your mother now, Marcus? Any idea?" Tommy asked.

"Yeah, she's um . . . staying in some homeless shelter for women. That's all I've been told. That she doesn't want anybody to see her until she gets herself together. And she's been getting herself together for *fifteen years* now. She didn't even make it to my younger brother's funeral."

Tommy shook his head. "Man, I'm sorry to hear that. But, despite it all, you still turned out pretty good, Marcus."

"At this point, Tommy, I've accepted it. You never know what life has in store for you. The drug dealer, or whoever got my mother strung out, that person doesn't understand all the lives they destroy, or the families they tear apart. My mom made some bad choices. Probably got hooked up with the wrong people, hanging in the wrong circles. I still forgive her, though. But as far as I'm concerned . . . that's my mother asleep in that bedroom right there. That is the woman who raised me."

Marcus threw his arm around me and dropped a kiss on the crown of my head. "That is exactly why I love you, Lula." His eyes locked on mine. "We have more in common than most people realize. I'd even go as far as to say that we might be soul mates!"

All of us laughed. But I was surprised more than anything. Because this was the first time I'd heard Marcus use the word love associated with my name in the same sentence. This was the first time he'd shown that type of affection in front of our friends. I felt the same way about him, felt our relationship ascending to another level. I also felt blessed to have a partner who understood what it was that I was fighting for. And how what I was doing often took away from time spent in each other's company.

Tommy slapped his hands on his knees and sat forward. "Well, we need to get home. Ariel's mother is watching the baby only up until her bedtime. She has a high school reunion breakfast in the morning."

Marcus and I stood up and walked Ariel and Tommy to the door. After a huge group hug, Marcus turned on the porch light and held open the screen door. "We'll wait for you to get in your car. Because both of you *know* you shouldn't be on this side of town after dark. Carjackings have almost *tripled* in the past three years!" he said.

I gave Marcus a playful shot to the arm. Then

we waved goodbye as Ariel and Tommy backed out of the driveway and onto Michigan Avenue. After their car went in reverse in an attempt to head north, it suddenly stopped. The passenger side window lowered, and Tommy, now a silhouette against the moonless dark, leaned over. "It's not just the South Side these days, bro. It's going on everywhere!" After that, he smiled as he and Ariel sped down the street and disappeared into the night.

CHAPTER 10

I HAD ARRIVED home after a long day's work. First, there were classes, followed by meetings with the parents of kids who were said to have severe behavioral problems. For most of my time spent on the clock, even without a chance to eat, I tried to mediate a solution between the school's administration and the parents of these students. Because the last thing I wanted to see was for these children to be put on some type of psychotropic medication.

No sooner than I could get in my bedroom, strip off my clothes, my cell phone started buzzing with texts. My first thought was to ignore them. But what if it was something to do with one of my students? When I picked up my phone and looked at its screen, I saw a picture of Pastor Tompkins lying in a hospital bed. Mama D. was at his side, her hands airborne over his body—a pained look on her face.

I rushed into my mother's room, where she had been ironing her clothes for work. "I just got a text from Marcus. Pastor Tompkins is in the hospital. It looks really serious." I held up my phone to show my mother the picture.

She set the iron upright on the ironing board and came over to look at my phone. "That looks serious, baby girl. Why he looks unconscious!" Mama glanced up from looking at the phone's screen. "The look on his face reminds me of the look I saw on Ms. Martha's face as she laid on her deathbed."

"We need to get over to the hospital right away," I said. Mama unplugged the iron, and then we grabbed our coats and headed over to Jackson Southland Hospital. When we arrived in his room, he still looked asleep. A nurse stood on the side of his bed filling an IV bag with fluid. "My shifts over in forty-five minutes. But I'll be back to check on him before I leave." She closed the curtain separating Pastor Tompkins's bed from that of an elderly patient next to him.

Mama D. nodded to acknowledge me and Mama's presence. Then she lowered her head like she was fighting an army of emotions. "Lord, I knew they were gonna come at some point. I knew that his faith and his will would be tested by the *devil himself.*"

Suddenly I was made of stone. I struggled to comprehend exactly what Marcus's grandmother had been trying to say, what this was all about. I pulled him outside into the hall to get a better understanding. "What's going on? What happened to him?"

"They think he had a stroke?"

"A stroke?"

"Yeah. Mama D. said that Pastor Tompkins has been under a lot of stress lately, Lula." Marcus then turned to me from looking down the hall. "Not only is he being investigated for the misuse of church funds. Some local alderman is spurring an inquiry into First Deliverance's finances. But he's also being accused of sexual misconduct. Mama D. said that one of the church's secretaries is trying to blackmail him. She said that she and Pastor Tompkins have been carrying on a secret relationship that only the two of them knew about. Oh, and she also claims to be pregnant with his baby." Marcus shook his head. "Mama D. said that the church has been losing a lot of money, as well as its members."

My cheeks flushed. I stood there combing through the tangle of my thoughts. I didn't know whether or not to believe any of it. I remembered Cora, one of the slaves that worked in the big house who had snuck one of the bibles outside and gave it to Mama and me. I remember Mama and five other slaves huddled together in our cabin, cowering in fear as we studied God's word. I remembered me reciting verses because I was the only one who knew how to read, courtesy of my secret reading lessons with Ms. Martha. I thought of scripture and how we all fall short of the glory. I knew that regardless of what happened in Pastor Tompkins's life, that deep down he was a man of good intent. He was trying to make more of a difference—and now—he was apparently paying for it.

Marcus and I walked back into the room. We saw Mama D. and my mother, one on each side of the bed, gently speaking. Mama D. took in a deep breath and leaned back in her chair. She nodded her head forward. "Lula, I know how much it means to have the Pastor helping you in your move-ment. But I think its time for him to step down and let someone else take the reins." She glanced at

Pastor Tompkins. "That includes him stepping down from the church, too."

"Yes. No, I completely agree with you. How is he at this point? What's his prognosis?"

"They said that he should be okay. Might need some therapy, though. The doctor said that had that ambulance not gotten there as quick as it did, Pastor Tompkins would not have made it. It happened this morning. The police showed up at the church, walked into Pastor's office and placed him right under arrest. Before that, he had received a letter and then a call from our local alderman's office about how they were getting ready to investigate not only the church's finances, but Pastor's personal finances as well. If you ask me this is nothing more than a *witch hunt!*"

I glanced at Pastor Tompkins as he lay peacefully. His eyes were closed, his breathing barely noticeable. I didn't know if he could hear our conversation or if he even knew we were in the room. I was surprised to see that no one else had come, no family, no friends, except for some members of the congregation who said that they were on their way.

"They should arrest that woman, making such accusations. If it *were* true, if she was sleeping with him and got pregnant, that's bad in and of itself. So for the life of me . . . I can't understand why she would turn around and blackmail him," Mama D. went on.

Marcus shrugged. "That's the way of the world today, grandma. Everybody's looking for an easy way to come up. *Especially* the groupies and the gold diggers."

"Well, she'll soon find out that she's barking up the wrong tree. Pastor Tompkins knows some awfully good lawyers. And one of them is a member of the church," Mama D. replied.

Marcus nodded. "I remember him. He was the attorney who Pastor Tompkins brought with him when I got arrested at the Black Lives Matter protest downtown. He told me that he was a graduate of Yale. I was really impressed with him and his credentials."

My mother glanced up. "The woman who's accusing him of these terrible things . . . is that the same woman he brought with him to your house when you invited us over for the Fourth of July, Delores?"

"Huh? No, ma'am. The woman accusing him merely worked at the church. And if my memory serves correct, she's only been there for about eleven months. It just goes to show . . . you never know what motivations people have. I'm hoping that he'll be healthy enough to face these allegations without it taking him to an early grave!"

The doctor walked in the room. The four of us looked up, concerned with what he had to say. "Are you family?" he asked.

"No. Well, I guess you could say we're his church family," Mama D. said.

The doctor walked over behind Mama D., checking a reading on one of the monitors.

Mama D. took in a deep breath. "I know it's kind of early to tell, doctor. But in your expert opinion, do you think he's going to be okay? We're not ready to lose him just yet."

"When he came in earlier he was in pretty bad shape. He had blurred vision and was apparently very confused. What he suffered is called a transient ischemic attack. Or in laymen's terms a mini-stroke. While not generally considered to be as detrimental as a regular stroke, a small percentage of patients will go on to have some permanent damage."

The doctor began writing something on Pastor Tompkins's chart.

"All we can do is pray for him. And hope that

he'll return to his usual upbeat self," my mother said.

The doctor glanced up. "Just to piggyback on what I said earlier, which is . . . it's possible that he'll fully recover. But he still may experience some lingering short-term effects. They brought him in after he suffered the stroke en route to the police station. There are still several policemen here at the hospital. If things had been a lot worse, he'd be in the ICU. He's still going to need ongoing care and support once he's discharged. Hopefully, someone, a close friend or relative, or even any of you, can be there for him once he's released."

"We will, and we'll be praying for him too," all of us said simultaneously.

"Good. I'll be back to check on him." The doctor smiled, and then he left the room.

Mama D. clasped her hands in front of her and leaned forward. She stared at Marcus, and me, and also at Mama as she apparently sought to gather her thoughts. "I want to say how proud I am of all of you, and that includes you too, Ella Mae." I saw my mother flash a smile of appreciation as Mama D. ventured into one of her prized teachable moments. "Don't any of you get discouraged. Not now. This battle is yours to win. The everyday working class. You know, I'd be out there with you if I were about fifty years younger. But all I can do now is root for you from the sidelines, and from the comfort of my own living room. I see the progress that you young folks are making, and it truly puts a smile on my face. Reminds me of the progress that was achieved, little by little, during the time I was your age. Each generation has to do *their* part to move the needle forward." Mama D. then swiveled her gaze toward the bed. "And I'm sure Pastor Tompkins would agree with me."

My cell phone buzzed in my purse. At this point, I didn't want to talk to anyone for fear of hearing something else that might be painful to accept. But I pulled it out anyway and saw that it was a text from Father Bigos. Apparently, he had gotten word of Pastor Tompkins being in the hospital. He wanted to let everyone know that he was praying for a speedy recovery. That he would be here to visit within the next twenty-four hours. 'Thanks for your concern. We will definitely keep you posted' I texted back. He replied thanking us, and then added:

Do not let the one whose job it is to kill, steal, and destroy, keep you from fulfilling the destiny that God has for you.

After that, there was an emoticon, a yellow smiley face.

Mama D. rested her hands on top of her cane. "As soon as I get home I'm going to call that criminal defense attorney. I'm not going to let them ruin everything that Pastor Tompkins has worked for all these years. All that he's done in the Bronzeville community. All that he's trying to do to help young people from poor neighborhoods get on their feet— all over some trumped up charges."

I hated to see Mama D. get so emotionally worked up at her age. But I had to completely agree with her. The only way to come out of this—for all of us—was to simply fight. Because if we didn't fight at the earliest signs of adversity, then we would all fall like dominoes. The Movement would become a social topic of what could have been, of what once was. A blip on the radar of human history. That was something I honestly hoped I would never have to see. Not ever. The other thing none of us wanted to see was Pastor Tompkins get railroaded into oblivion.

CHAPTER 11

Ariel's parents invited Mama and me to their house on a Saturday evening. It was the first time we'd been to their home in a long time. Every time I would set foot in their condo, it brought back a flood of memories. Being there was the first time I'd experienced living in any type of a humane environment. Sometimes I even thought . . . *what if.* What if Ariel had not found me disoriented on the street that day, and I had to remain homeless.

Homeless in an unknown world, over a hundred years into the future.

When we stepped inside Ariel was busy washing a load of clothes. Patty, her mother, was in the kitchen cooking up one of her fabulous meals. And her father, Randy, was in their bedroom downloading something on his computer. Mama and I walked into the living room and sat on the sofa.

"Hey, thanks for coming, Lula, Ella Mae. Sorry to hear about your Pastor being in the hospital. We're praying that he makes a speedy recovery. Strokes are very serious."

I nodded. "Thank you. Everyone around me has been under a lot of pressure and stress. But we will continue the good fight." Ariel came into the living room and gave Mama and me a hug. Trailing close behind her was Thomas Jr., rolling across the carpet in a blue baby walker.

"Tommy had to work unexpectedly. He thinks his boss is punishing him for calling off last week. But he told me to tell you all hello."

Randy came walking into the room holding a can of Coors light. "Hello ladies, good to see you brave the weather so that you could join us." He walked around the cocktail table and then sat on the end of the sofa, near Mama. He leaned back and turned on the television mounted on the wall. "It's just the six of us. That said, tonight should be a *normal* getting together among family. The only reason I say that is because my brother won't be here being his usual goofball self. If he *were* here . . . we'd have to hide the Jack Daniels."

We all laughed. I remembered Ariel's uncle and how he was the life of the party at her housewarming. I also remembered her aunt Gertie and how she seemed so out of touch with the real world.

"Lula, a little off topic here, but I figure there's no better time to say this than the present. You know we've always been proud of everything you stand for. But I've been growing more and more concerned about you lately. Concerned about all of you, actually," Randy said.

Patty walked into the room with a vegetable tray and set it on the table. "Make that both of us. People can label us conspiracy nuts all they want, but sometimes there is truth in what's being said. And I agree that the timing of what's happening to your pastor sounds extremely suspicious."

As Ariel stood listening intently, her son rammed his walker into the back of her leg. She looked down at her baby as he tried to circle her body. I'm sure that he was merely trying to get her attention. "I think he's trying to put me on disability so that I'll constantly be home with him," she said amusingly.

"You did the same when you were a kid," Patty said. Ariel smiled. "No I didn't."

"Yes, you did. You probably don't remember.

You had this crazy habit of pulling down books and magazines off the shelves. Anything that wasn't glued or nailed down was fair game to be *yanked* onto the floor. It didn't bother us though. We thought it was hilarious."

Mama chimed in. "Being a parent *does* require patience. Kids are always going to get into mischief and play. But lately, there's been so much tragedy in the news having to do with parents and their children. I told Lula that I'm going to stop watching it. It's too depressing."

Ariel leaned over and picked up her baby from his walker. "Well, I'd rather keep up with what's going on in the world. On channel five they even mentioned the allegations concerning Pastor Tompkins."

Randy set his beer down on the table and rested his elbows on his knees. He shifted his gaze around the room. "I think I've lived long enough to read between the lines. And I can plainly see what's going on here. I think it's time I get more involved."

"Dad, how do you mean?" Ariel asked.

"Well, I can't sit by and see any of you put yourself in a tough situation and not help. I was always brought up with a mindset of being of service to others. Ariel, I don't know if I've ever told you this story. But when I was a kid my father took us to see the Brewers play when we had lived in Milwaukee. On our way home my father wanted to stop by a convenience store. Outside the store was a homeless man, disheveled, tattered clothes, sitting underneath an awning on the sidewalk. He had asked my father if he could spare any change. So my dad reached into his pocket and showed the guy a fifty-dollar bill. My dad told him that it could be used for his benefit on the condition that it was not spent on alcohol. And to make sure of it, my dad and I had the man follow us across the street to a department store. My dad bought him some clothes, and then a hot meal from the cafeteria in the store. I'll never forget the smile on that man's face, and how grateful he was." Ariel's father glanced at his wife, then at Mama and me. "We've got some extra money set aside. And I've got resources around town within the ranks of city government. I want us to help with your Movement, however we can. Because I know there will be a lot of folks being helped in the process. This has nothing to do with color or political affiliation. This is simply about people helping other people."

Mama shifted. "Mr. Evans, you and your family have already done so much for us. Quite a bit. And we're forever grateful. But we *don't* want to get you involved not knowing what lies ahead."

"Ella Mae, Lula, I'm afraid you won't be able to talk me out of it. Besides, they already know who I am. I'm sure I'm already on their radar concerning our pledge to keep both of your pasts a secret."

Patty stood up from the couch. "We can continue our conversation over dinner. It's finally ready, and I don't want the food getting cold."

Mama and I took turns washing our hands in the bathroom. Then we joined Ariel, her parents, and Thomas Jr. at the kitchen table.

"Everything's organic, no GMOs," Ariel's mother said as she set down a platter of smothered chicken.

Mama turned toward me. "What's GMOs?"

"It's a way of manipulating food through genetic engineering, Mama. GMO stands for Genetically Modified Organism. It's something I don't care to eat. That's why I look at the labels when I go shopping."

"Oh, well I guess that explains it," my mother replied.

"Explains what?" I asked.

Mama glanced up at me. "That explains why

some of the food we been eating don't taste like it did over a hundred and fifty years ago. In 1852."

Ariel chuckled as her parents exchanged a concerned glance. I shook my head. My mother could be funny even when she wasn't trying to be. I wondered if her next gig could be as a stand up comic. "Yeah, well, you might not want to mention that outside of our little circle here, Ella Mae," Randy mused. "With that being said, I would like for us to propose a toast to making a difference in the gone-to-crap world we read about every day!"

Randy stood up, grabbed an electric bottle opener from the drawer next to the refrigerator, and then popped the cork on a bottle of champagne. Then he poured each of us a half-filled glass. I watched as the bubbles fizzed. Other than Joe Gatlin's birthday party, this would be the only time I'd had an alcoholic drink. I wondered if this would be my first go-around with getting drunk.

"I did the toast last time." Randy held up his glass and jerked his chin. "Ella Mae? Care to do the honors tonight?"

Mama smiled. She set her fork down beside her plate. "Okay. All right. You asked me to say some-thing, so I'm going to tell you what I'd like to see happen. I'd like to see black folks, people of color,

and anyone else getting the short end of the stick . .
. to get their just due. I look around at how some of
us live in some of these neighborhoods, and other
than us running around as free men and women, to
be honest, I don't see a whole lot of progress.
Certainly not a whole century and a half worth. But I have
faith in God, you see, faith in my daughter, and
faith that all of us can do our part to bring about
change. It ain't going to happen overnight. And it
ain't going to happen without somebody putting in
the work that needs to be done." She lifted her glass
over the middle of the table. "Be that as it may, I
truly believe it can happen in my lifetime. So I'd like
to propose a toast with some words from a favorite
song of mine by Mr. Sam Cooke. It's been a long
time coming. But I know a change is gonna come."
Mama panned around our faces, pinning us with
her gaze. "That's what I would like to see happen
before I die. Because the world needs it now more
than ever. There's so much sin taking place. So
much immorality. The world needs to turn itself
back to God."

The five of us clinked glasses. "Amen," I said
and nodded.

CHAPTER 12

Mama D. urged all of us to be there for Pastor Tompkins the day he was released from the hospital. I imagined that with us being around him, and with him being in familiar surroundings, it would work wonders to brighten up his spirits. After I got dressed, I drank my usual cup of decaffeinated green tea. Then I rummaged through a file cabinet where documents about the Movement had been privately kept. I was excited to share some of the latest progress we had made in our fight to bring jobs and a thriving economy to some of the poorest neighborhoods in the city.

Mama and I started toward Marcus's house, first passing an early morning contingent of young men huddled on the corner. It was the same corner where a young man had gotten shot and killed in front of a liquor store in broad daylight. I still remember his lifeless body, the outpouring of cries from his mother's pain.

When we arrived at Mama D.'s house, she was putting the last bit of seasonings in a pot of hot gumbo. She'd always cooked with no salt, but somehow was able to do it where you wouldn't even notice. After she was done cooking, I watched her as she poured most of it inside of a Tupperware container. Gumbo was Pastor Tompkins's favorite meal. And I wasn't sure if he'd been given the ok to eat it. But everyone seemed adamant that it would be his first meal at home since being discharged.

The four of us rode in my car to the minister's house. It was a modest one-story brown brick bungalow just east of Stony Island Avenue in the Pill Hill neighborhood on the South Side. I was told that the name Pill Hill came about because of the large number of doctors that resided in the community during the 70s.

We arrived, parked directly behind a pair of Reserved Parking Handicap signs, and then got out of the car. With me on one side helping her maintain her balance, Mama D. grabbed the porch's black railing. And with Marcus holding the pot of gumbo the four of us went up the steps and rang the bell. The door opened wide, and smiling while pushing open the screen door was Ms. Mary, Pastor Tompkins's longtime appointed church cook. "Hello, church family. Pastor will be delighted to see you here." Ms. Mary leaned over and whispered, "Actually, I didn't tell him that you were coming. I wanted it to be a surprise."

Marcus handed her the pot of gumbo. And she took it into the kitchen to set it down. The living room was nicely decorated with clean beige carpet, a dark brown recliner, a flat screen TV, and a picture of Dr. Martin Luther King Jr. during one of his peace marches over a brick fireplace. A few second later, Ms. Mary came out of the kitchen and waved us to follow her into Pastor Tomkins's bedroom.

He shifted his gaze from watching a basketball game to us as we walked through the doorway. On the screen, some cheerleaders were dancing toward the court right before halftime. "Well, look what the cat drug in! Now I know I'm in good hands. Good to see you, Delores. Good to see all of you."

Mama D. leaned over to give him a hug, followed by Marcus, Mama and me. "Good to see you too, L.C. You know we had to come check on you. I made you some homemade gumbo. Ms.

Mary's got it in the kitchen." Mama D. studied him from head to toe as he lay. "Well, you definitely *look* good."

Pastor Tompkins pushed himself higher against his headboard. "You know, I feel so much better. And it's only by the grace of God I was able to come home this early. My doctor tells me that so far, there aren't any lingering effects, such as having weakness on one side or slurred speech."

My mother nodded. "That's good to hear, Pastor. We look forward to having you back in the pulpit as soon as you're feeling up to it."

Pastor Tompkins shrugged. "Well, I can tell you one thing . . . you really find out who your friends are when you go through hard times."

"Care to elaborate?" said Mama D.

The pastor shook his head. "As you all can see, my lady friend, you know, the one I brought to your house on the holiday, Delores? She's nowhere to be found now. Ever since this scandal hit and I got sick, she no longer returns any of my calls."

Mama D. shook her head. "That doesn't surprise me one bit. People are only out for them-selves these days, Pastor. They're only out for what they can get out of others. But it is a good thing your eyes were opened early on before you got in too deep with that woman."

"I hope you all know I didn't do the things that they're accusing me of. As soon as I get on my feet, I'm going to fight these charges *vigorously*."

Marcus smiled. "We've got your back, Pastor Tompkins. Mama D. has already contacted the attorney who attends the church. The one that graduated from Yale."

"I'll tell you what *I* believe. I believe that some group or entity has infiltrated the church! None of this stuff occurred before I got involved with the Movement. Now I'm not saying that to point any fingers or to make excuses. Because I believe in what you young people are doing! And I'm going to *continue* to do my part."

Ms. Mary brought in a bowl of Mama D.'s seafood gumbo along with some French bread and a light green salad. She set a breakfast tray in front of Pastor Tompkins as he prepared to eat. "Speaking of the Movement, how are things going? I haven't heard much about it since I've been on the mend."

I opened a manila folder and pulled out a document on which I'd been tracking our progress. It contained important dates, milestones as each of our goals had been reached, and names of key contacts of the companies that we'd decided to boycott.

"First, in the last month, there have been over five thousand jobs created in the inner city. This was due in part to Ariel's father's company putting pressure on one of its suppliers to relocate their manufacturing facility here. Second, we've been given a firm commitment by a large grocery chain to open some of their new stores in impoverished neighborhoods, so that nearby residents can have fresh produce, something other than the fast food and fried chicken places on every corner."

Pastor Tompkins flashed a toothy grin. "This is like music to my ears, Lula. Please, keep going."

"Third, according to our latest statistics, police-involved shootings of unarmed minorities across the country is now at an all-time low, due mainly to increased accountability and oversight. Fourth, we are expecting, by the end of the quarter, to have better censorship of television programs, video games, and movies. Because we have an online petition of parents across the country, approximately seven hundred thousand names thus far, who have agreed to boycott any TV station and film studio, which has been recognized as needing increased programming classified as being family-friendly. And lastly, wherever possible, we have made a concerted effort to have belief in God, as well as prayer, implemented back into elementary, middle-grade, and high schools." I glanced up from reading. "Most of the schools in the communities we're trying to help—have no problem with this."

Pastor Tompkins grinned broadly. He set his tray on the nightstand beside his bed. "Lula, I'm so proud of what you all have accomplished, my dear sister. You all have already taken the torch handed off by my generation, and ran farther with it than I ever thought could be possible. Especially in such a relatively short period of time. Please tell Ariel and her family how much I appreciate the work they're putting in as well."

I nodded. "This is only a start. There's still a lot of work to be done. The good news is that other urban centers are seeing what is possible. And many are implementing their own boycotts and strategies for real change."

"Well, it's a mighty fine start. Because people, our folks, in particular, don't recognize the economic buying power they have until it's put to good use!" Pastor Tompkins announced.

"Lula, you forgot to tell him about the big-time rally we have planned next week!" said Marcus.

I smiled. "We've got a rally planned in downtown Chicago. I think it's going to be our biggest yet."

Pastor Tompkins nodded and smiled. "That's good stuff. And I sure wish I could be there with you, my sister. Will it be televised? If so, I'll definitely be watching."

"We've been told to expect at least the local media," I replied.

"Well, please, keep safety and security a major concern. I've seen chaos and violence at other rallies around the country. I'm hoping things don't get out of hand. There's nothing wrong with a peaceful protest. It's our right to do so as Americans." Pastor Tompkins raised his arm and motioned us to move closer. "Please come, family, I'd like for us to bow our heads in prayer right here in this room. You know, the enemy is always working. Now that change is taking place, and good work is being done, you can count on the enemy of God doing his best to thwart our plans!"

We walked forward, closer to Pastor Tompkins's bed. We held hands and bowed our heads in prayer. As Pastor T. recited Psalm 23 verse 4 from the King

James Bible, I literally concentrated on every word. Because I knew the extraordinary power that prayer wielded. And had seen it work ever since I was a little girl in the antebellum South. I also knew that as time went on, as more change was being implemented around the country, that I would be forced to live under a microscope of public opinion.

I thought of civil rights icons that worked on behalf of our people laying the groundwork on which I now stood. I thought of the danger they'd put themselves in to see the change which was necessary at the time. I thought of Dr. Martin Luther King Jr.'s "I Have a Dream" speech during the march on Washington in 1963. And I had to ask myself was I willing to die for the cause to make this world a better place, not only for those who live today, but for the generations of tomorrow, too.

With Mama's help and the help of my team, we worked diligently and tirelessly over the next seven days so that our rally could be a success. I conducted numerous phone interviews with journalists, made appointments with city officials, and had meetings with various groups. Soon I'd learned that because of the buzz that had been generated, and the number of people that were expected at the event, that CNN would be covering it live.

I received a firm commitment from, Darius, the ex-con who lived in the halfway house on the West Side, that he would talk to the gang members he knew about joining our efforts. I'd also accepted a handshake promise from Larone Toobin, the currently incarcerated gang leader who called for a cease-fire, and an opportunity for his members to hear our plan for their economic involvement, so that they could put down their guns and pick up a marketable skill instead.

Before I went to bed, I turned on my computer to check my email. The first message I saw was from Father Bigos. He wanted me to have a list of the various groups and entities that had planned on protesting at our rally. As I perused the list, I quickly noticed that some of them were known hate groups. Some of which promised to make our event a living hell. What that meant exactly, I wasn't sure. But I knew that it meant there was a good chance of violence in the forecast. Father Bigos ended his message by saying, *He wanted me to know what we were up against so that we could be prepared.*

I felt a knot in the back of my throat. For the

first time since I'd first started the Movement, I felt fear wash over me like a tide washes along the shore. I immediately charged into my mother's room.

"I'm not sure I can go through with this. Father Bigos sent me an email warning of the threats we face at the rally, Mama."

My mother patted the empty space next to her as she sat on her bed. "Sit right here," she said. Then she pulled me into her embrace, my head buried in her neck. "You've come a long way, baby girl. You've got a lot of people counting on you. Thousands if not millions. Can't give up the dream now." My mother pulled away from me so that we were now eye to eye. "Go ahead and accomplish what you've set out to do, Lula. The world, and hurting people everywhere—will be better for it."

I smiled. My mother always knew how to make me better, more confident, feel brighter, even when the road to be traveled had seemed its darkest. Still somewhat shaken and unsure, "but what if I can't," I said.

My mother put her finger to my lips. "But what if you *can*," she assured. "Your daddy used to say that God put the seed of courageousness inside of you. One night, while everyone was asleep in our

cabin, you, me, your daddy, Clarence, were all startled when an overseer, and Mr. Mansfield, and two
other men stormed into our quarters. A young boy
belonging to the Gaines family next door had been
found along a creek. After a long search through the
woods, they discovered his bloodied body lying on a
chunk of petrified wood. They believed he had
been killed by one of the slaves. So an order was
given to round up the field hands that had lived
closest to where the body was found. When the
overseer raised his fist in the air striking your father,
because he screamed he knew nothing about the
boy's death, you reached down, grabbed a stick,
and with all your might, swung it mercilessly,
striking the legs of the overseer!"

"I don't remember that. I imagine I must have
made things worse for you and Daddy?"

"They allowed us to go back to our cabin. But
for several months they terrified every slave who
worked anywhere near where the boy was found.
Word had it that one of the Gaines's own slaves had
been charged with the murder."

I took a deep breath. "It's still hard for me to
believe that I've gotten myself into this much
responsibility at my age."

Mama grabbed my arm. "Listen to me, it is *our*

time now! Our time to rise from the depths of oppression to our rightful place in God's grand scheme of things. And it's obvious that God chose you to be a catalyst for the change that has got to come! So I say . . . *rise up*, and fulfill the purpose that God has anointed over your life!"

I leaned over and kissed my mother on the cheek. She always knew exactly how to lift me when I was down. How to instill confidence when I had become wary of what paths to follow. "Thank you, Mama," I said. As I stood to leave her room, I turned around and smiled. Mama's eyes trailed me as I walked through the doorway and then went to my room. Once inside, I slipped out of my clothes, into my nightgown, and then lay upon a sea of pillows. I reached over, pulling open the drawer to my nightstand, and proceeded to read, "Where Do We Go From Here: Chaos or Community" by Dr. Martin Luther King Jr.

In some ways, I felt like history was repeating itself. But I was determined that more be done, more progress be made—to move the needle on the odometer of history and humankind forward. After reading, I went to sleep on a hope and a prayer.

CHAPTER 13

MILLENIUM PARK, Chicago, IL

I went over the words in my mind. Words I hoped would not only make a difference to people here tonight, but would explain why the Movement was so absolutely necessary. Before the first speaker was scheduled to come up, I looked out from behind the podium. I saw a sea of people that had swelled to numbers that were unimaginable even two months ago. I waved down the side of my hair as the wind gusted off the lake. The air was crisp and cold, a bite like the start of winter. Glancing at the darkening sky, I noticed seagulls swooping down in search of food. Were they simply hungry? Or was it God's way of sending a sign that there could be trouble brewing. In front of me, I estimated, were at least five to seven hundred people, with more steadily coming in by the busloads.

This was diversity. This was the flip side of segregation with a common goal in mind.

I noticed whites, blacks, Latinos, all of various ages. Among them were Mama, Marcus, Ariel and her parents, Ju Ju Gatlin and Darius, the ex-gang member and convicted felon from the halfway house. On each side of the crowd and directly in front of it were the media, including CNN. Off to the side, forming a human barricade and watching intently was Chicago police. Most of them on foot and some on horses.

Several community activists, local, and from New York and Los Angeles, were scheduled to speak before me. So with thirty minutes to go before I took center stage, I sat facing the crowd, which had been steadily growing by the minute. I watched as a man by the name of Dr. Malik Osborne-Ali walked up and started addressing the crowd about the need for economics, the need for better jobs, higher wages, decent housing, and quality education. I had heard about Malik from Father Bigos, how he was instrumental in helping the Bed Stuy section of Brooklyn become more economically viable during the 70s and 80s. So I was excited to have him here to share his knowledge, experience, and results.

Standing at the front of the crowd in clerical attire was Father Bigos. He was flanked on his right by his security team, and on his left by Jay Killa, his entourage, and a photog from his music label, Mystère Records. To their left was Marcus and Mama, Ariel and her parents. Marcus smiled, nodded, and then pointed to me as if giving a non-verbal command for me to absolutely *own it!*

But just as Father Bigos had warned, there was an increasing amount of anti-protestors, White Nationalists, some holding confederate flags, some with posters with swastikas painted on them. There was a fenced barricade set up to separate them from those supporting the Movement. Their yells and shouts of self-preservation began to drown out Malik's finishing statements. Malik, standing onstage in a black wool coat, and wearing a kufi cap made of colorful kente cloth—finished by raising his fist prominently in the air.

When he left the podium, I was given the signal to go up and speak. I imagined that the police, as well as our own security had been growing increas-ingly concerned. I stepped up and adjusted the microphone to the sound of cheers and chants of encouragement. Cameramen from the local media and CNN moved closer to the stage.

"Thank you! Because of you, we are making a *difference!*" I smiled as I pointed out to the crowd. I saw Mama, Marcus, Ariel and her parents applauding and giving each other high fives. I continued. "Because of *you*, we have helped to shatter the longstanding systems of division, oppression, and racism. Because of *you*, the obstacles that have kept the American Dream out of reach for so many—regardless of race, have now been broken— the same obstacles that for generations have supported the foundations of injustice and inequality!" There were cheers followed by a brief pause. My eyes welled as a strong wind gusted from the east.

"No, because of you, my son will have a better future and be able to attend better schools right here in Chicago," a white man pointed and shouted from the audience. He was standing next to a black woman who I assumed to be his wife, or perhaps his partner. He was holding a boy on his shoulders that looked biracial.

Suddenly one of the white nationalists yelled a racial slur. There was pushing and shoving as a throng of the Movement's supporters made there way over to where the two groups had been separated. A CNN reporter was shoved out of the way.

"Please, let's do this peacefully. We can disagree without resorting to violence," I yelled from the stage. I had seen fights break out in other cities at rallies for other causes. The last thing I wanted was for the same to occur here tonight. Because I knew that it would give our cause a bad name. I knew that if things got out of hand, it could be used to prevent us from having rallies in the future. But fights and skirmishes broke out between the two factions. I looked out near the front of the crowd and saw Randy and Marcus trying to get Mama, Ariel and her mother away to safety.

The police were outnumbered as they tried to maintain order. Rocks and bottles were thrown, some onstage. As the entire crowd of supporters and anti-demonstrators neared the stage, I grew more concerned that someone would be seriously hurt, or perhaps even killed.

I searched for a way to exit the platform safely. But out of the corner of my eye, I saw hundreds of people flee in sheer panic. Someone in a black SUV came barreling through the crowd and toward the stage. The only thing I remembered seeing was the headlights of the vehicle as it sped through the masses of people. Whoever was driving had accelerated at full speed with no regard for human life. Darius, who was standing near the side of the platform, lunged and yanked me off stage and onto the ground. We both fell onto the pavement with me on top of him, disoriented.

The SUV crashed into the stage in a horrible crunch of metal. I saw a group of policemen rush to the vehicle with their guns drawn. They broke the glass and then yanked out the driver, a bald white man with neck and facial tattoos, onto the ground. "Lula, you all right?" Darius asked. Everything had happened so fast. I was still trying to make some kind of sense of it all. In the back of my mind, I knew that there was the potential for violence. But not once did I expect things to descend to this level of madness. "Yeah. I'm okay," I responded. Darius gently rolled me off him so that we could both get on our feet. I wondered what had happened to Mama, to Marcus, to Ariel and her parents. Before I could wipe the dust and debris from my clothes, I found myself on the ground again, this time face down. "What's going on?" I yelled as my cheek was pinned to the pavement.

"You're under arrest for mob action!" A police

officer's command was the only thing I'd heard save for the busy chatter from the small radio on his chest. I looked over at Darius who had also been wrestled to the ground; his hands were placed behind his back. Next, I heard the distinctive clink of cuffs as they were placed around his wrists, then mine. The cop who had thrown me down then jerked me to my feet.

"Man this is a bunch of B.S. How you gonna blame us for this?" Darius cried. After getting upright, he stared down the cop who had arrested him. For several seconds they locked onto each other's gaze. As the officer began walking him forward, Darius started jerking his body in an act of defiance. "I ain't going back to jail, man. This don't make no sense!"

I looked over at him. "Darius, it's going to be okay. Please, just comply. Don't make it worse. We'll work our way through this." I could only imagine the fear that must have coursed through him. Because Darius already had several strikes against him, if any of these charges were to stick, he could be looking at doing serious time. "Don't do the crime if you can't do the time," one of the cops countered. To the shock and horror of bystanders, the police escorted us away from Millennium Park and into one of many waiting squad cars. I turned and looked around. There was no sign of Mama, Marcus, Ariel and her parents or Father Bigos. It was a blessing that neither Mama D. nor Pastor Tompkins had been in any type of condition to be here. But I'm sure they had to have seen the chaos unfold on TV. I'm sure they were on pins and needles worried about our safety.

The ride on the way to the station had become a very familiar one. While sitting in the back of the squad car I thought of the people I held in high regard. The civil rights icons in the past, American heroes like, Rosa Parks, and how she, like others, had decided to stand up courageously for what was right and proper—regardless of the outcome. When we arrived at 1st District headquarters and taken inside, one of the first cops to see me was the one who had fingerprinted me when I was arrested at Father Bigos's church. He was sipping from a Styrofoam cup. He smiled as I was being marched through the revolving glass door and then down a corridor.

"Just can't stay away, huh?" he said sarcastically.

I rounded on him. "No. This is what happens when you want your voice to be heard. Actually, I've got company this time, too." As me and the cop who had arrested me continued through the building, I noticed that for some strange reason I was being led into what looked like a large interrogation room instead of going through the usual booking process that I had gone through before. Another officer, a tall young looking cop with blond hair, pulled out a chair and I sat at the end of a square black table. Then a woman walked into the room holding a manila folder. She was model thin with shoulder-length black hair curled neatly at the bottom and was wearing dark sunglasses.

"Lula, I'm an agent with the National Security Agency. My name is Cheryl Del Priore. Mind if I have a seat?"

I nodded. "Please."

She opened the folder, then slid it to the side. It had the text: Classified, stamped on the front of it in bold red letters. After several seconds she closed it, then looked down at her watch.

"What is this about?" I asked.

"I'm waiting for some of my colleagues to get here." She tossed her hair away from her face. "You may not know who I am. But I'm quite familiar with who you are."

I stared at this woman and wondered what she could have meant. How much does she actually know about me? And what does she know about my past?

"Let me start out by saying that I know about the fascinating story concerning you and your mother. I've talked to your adoptive parents. I helped arrange the trip for you and your mother to go to Fort Meade," she said.

"Well, now I'm being targeted for something entirely different. All I want to do is help those who are less fortunate. I was arrested tonight at a rally for no reason other than for having a voice and speaking up."

Del Priore nodded. "I understand. But you also have to be cognizant of our concerns. This is a topic of national security."

I heard the room's door open. I glanced up and saw Marcus, Mama, Ariel and her parents. I stood up to hug each one of them.

My mother embraced me. "I was truly worried about you, baby girl. Worried that you would be trampled under that stage. Are you hurt?" she asked as I buried my head in her neck.

I looked up and shook my head. "My shoulder's a little sore. I've got some scratches on my face. But other than that, I'm okay."

Marcus wrapped me up in his arms. "Man, that

crowd went completely insane! They should've never let those white supremacists get that close to the stage! What were they thinking?"

Ariel and her mother pulled me into their embrace. "We've got to find a way of keeping you safe. It doesn't make sense that you're constantly putting your life in danger, Lula."

Randy gently rested the palm of his hand on the top my back. "Glad that you got out of there in time. I should have known that something was going to happen after that idiot yelled the racial slur! Who's this?" he asked.

The NSA agent removed her glasses. "Mr. Evans, Cheryl Del Priore. We met in your office some time ago," she said jutting out her hand.

"Yeah, I remember. You were with some other gentlemen. They were with the CIA. Agent Haupht, was it?"

Del Priore nodded. "That's correct. We were the ones initially assigned to this case. We have special orders to maintain contact with the family."

Randy shook his head. "I don't think I understand. We've complied with the government's orders. We haven't disclosed either Lula's or her mother's past to anyone."

Suddenly agent Haupht and another man came in the door shaking off an umbrella. I recognized him instantly, remembered his intense stare the night I met with federal agents recounting the moment I left Natchez Mississippi in 1854 and arrived on the South Side of Chicago as a free slave.

"Good to see you, folks, again," he said as he sat next to Del Priore. "I'm Special Agent Haupht with the CIA, and this is my colleague, Mr. Lester Donaldsen. Now you're probably wondering what this is all about—and why you're talking to us, Lula, instead of spending the night down the hall in a cell. Well, we're going to get to that in just a moment. First, let me say that I'm glad that you were not hurt this evening."

I nodded. "Thank you for your concern."

Agent Del Priore slid the manila folder in front of agent Haupht. He looked at us as if this were an important meeting in the Situation Room to decide whether or not to declare war on another country. "There's been a bombshell development," Haupht said as he removed a sheet from his stack of documents. He looked up. "Lula, the time machine that transported you and your mother from the past into the future? We've found out that it's *here*. It's here in the present—the present day, United States of America."

I looked at Mama, at Marcus, and at Ariel and her parents. We were all frozen, completely miffed at how this could be. "How is it here?" I asked, perplexed.

Agent Haupht slid a photograph across the table to where we were seated. "What we've been able to ascertain is that when your mother, Ella Mae, traveled through time, somehow, the machine came with her. We believe that whatever disc, or mechanism, was created by Hartley Mansfield, made it so that there were only two chances, or two attempts, left at traveling through time and space. That right there is believed to be a picture of it."

The six of us studied the image. I handed it off to Mama who then stared at it.

"Is that it?" Agent Haupht asked.

Mama and I nodded our heads. "Yes, that's it," Mama replied. "I remembered the shape of it, the color and how the disc slid into that narrow open-ing. And those words engraved on it's side. Just like I remember it," she said.

A million thoughts began to float through my consciousness. I wondered what the government was going to do with it. Try to reverse engineer it for the purpose of scientific research? Or possibly use it for some sinister purpose? "Where is it?" I asked.

"Yeah. And how did you find out about it?" Randy added.

Agent Haupht leaned back in his chair. "I thought you folks would like to know that. There was an unsolved murder in the area some time ago, which eventually turned into a cold case. One of the homicide detectives working the case decided to take another look at some surveillance footage from security cameras nearby. Detectives often do that for numerous reasons, maybe a hunch they'll find a new clue or some missing piece of evidence. So when the detective noticed in the distance something he described as strange, he shared the recording with his superiors, which led to the opening of a new investigation.

"So here's what apparently happened. When the transporter arrived with Ella Mae in it that morning on Chicago Avenue. A man by the name of Herman Archibald, an antiques dealer, saw it unattended on the sidewalk several doors down from his store. He, with the help of the store's manager, Paul Forsyth, lifted Ella Mae out of the machine while she was disoriented. Figuring that she was just another homeless person that no one would care about, they covered her body with trash bags they'd brought with them from the establishment. Then they placed it on top of a padded hardwood end dolly and rolled it into the store. Afterward, they just left her there.

"Mr. Archibald tried to sell it first on the black market, and then to a large antiquities dealer slash auction house, who in turn, alerted authorities that the item might have been stolen, especially with it having Hartley Mansfield's name engraved on its side." Haupht leaned forward. "But the bottom line is that we don't have it. A search warrant was obtained to search Archibald's place. And we came up empty," Haupht said as he clasped his fingers together on the table. "Which brings us to *you*. Archibald claims that the sweet little ol' black woman he'd found inside the Transporter that morning, namely—you, Ella Mae, came into his shop several months later, and took it off his hands for five hundred dollars cash."

Mama stood up. "That is a boldface *lie!* I did not do what that man is saying I did. Why I ain't seen that much money at one time since we been here!"

My neck flushed with heat. Pure panic crossed

over my mother's face. Immediately I reached out and held her arm, hoping that she would settle down. "We don't have the Transporter. If we did, we would have *told* you!" I said.

Randy interceded. "What proof do you have these ladies have it in their possession? Do you have Ella Mae on surveillance tape going into that place as you allege?"

Donaldsen unbuttoned his suit jacket and leaned back in his seat. "No. Per the business owner where the cameras are installed, there were some days when they, admittedly, were not working." He jerked his chin toward Mama. "But you work in that area. And you two are the only people outside of the federal government that actually *knows what that thing is capable of.* To anyone else, it's just an old box."

I shook my head. "At this point, my mother and I would have no interest in it. You couldn't possibly think that we would want to go back to living life as we knew it." I made sure to look at Agent Del Priore, pinning her with my gaze. Because I hoped that, woman-to-woman, there could be some common ground established between us. A morsel of compassion that could lead to some type of resolution here.

Del Priore removed her sunglasses and stared at Mama and me. "Look, we are prepared to make a deal."

"What kind of deal?" Randy asked.

"We need to find that machine. And we won't stop until it is found. The Transporter is not something we want falling into the wrong hands. God forbid if it were to end up in the possession of some rogue, or hostile nation. Can you imagine the implications? The possibility of going through time, and altering history? Or perhaps being able to change the outcome of certain events? Lula, the reality is . . . if you and your mother will simply come clean about its whereabouts, then we are prepared to drop the case the government has against you. But we need an answer. And we need it right here. Right now!"

"We are telling you the truth. We have nothing to hide," I answered nervously.

"Then I'm afraid we have no deal," Agent Del Priore replied. "You will remain in custody until such time a court date and trial can be afforded to you."

"Wait! What?" I blurted. Suddenly I was made of stone. The thought of me being incarcerated, once again having my freedom taken away, had quickly become a stark new reality. I looked at my mother as tears streamed down her cheeks, her face clotted with pain. I put my arm around her.

"You people can't do this!" Randy exploded. "You can't railroad her with these trumped up charges and expect them to stick! This is not the end! I will see to it, even if I have to hire every criminal defense lawyer in town, I'll do it. This is not the end of it!"

I watched as Ariel and her mother cried. Marcus leaned over and put his arms around Mama and me. Del Priore rose and jerked her chin toward the door, and two policemen came in. They grabbed my arm and pulled me to my feet. "Ms.?" one of them said, and he gestured toward the door.

"Don't worry, Lula! We will get you released!" Randy assured.

Those were the last words I heard as I was being escorted down the hallway. I was taken through an exit, which I imagined was for transporting inmates, then loaded into a van and carted off to another location. I thought of the progress we had made with the Movement. I thought about my friends and family and not ever being able to see them outside of the arranged visits every prisoner is given. I thought about Mama and how we've been inseparable through harrowing trials and tribulations— the kind most people could never fathom.

Once we'd arrived at the county jail, I was shuttled inside, then marched into a receiving area where I was checked for contraband, had my fingerprints and digital booking photo taken and issued a booking number. Then I was escorted down a corridor with a group of other women and into a room. A female corrections officer in a black uniform closed the door behind us. "Okay, this is a strip search. Everything comes off and remains in this room."

Embarrassed and humiliated, I reluctantly started to slip off my clothes. Because being naked, having to turn around and spread your cheeks, squat, cough—all the while feeling violated, was something I could never get used to.

After being given state-issued clothing, a set of bright yellow scrubs, I was led down a corridor, through a buzzed gate and to a holding cell where a female CO inserted a key and opened a steel door. "Go on," she said.

I went inside, and through a narrow piece of glass in the door's center, I watched her as she walked back down the hall. The sound of her shoes clapping against the tile was a distinct reminder of where I'd found myself, as was the sound of the cuffs and the keys jingling on her belt.

Inside the cell with me was a large black woman lying on a bunk, reading a newspaper. She glanced up as I stood in the middle of the floor holding my bedroll.

"I think they're finally going to legalize weed," she announced. "Can you believe it? After all this time. It's been a big money maker for other states."

"Well, how about they find a way to criminalize racism?" I countered.

She smiled. "Now *that* would be an absolute miracle!" She bolted upright on her bed. "Hey, what are you in for? You look like you've never committed a crime in your life."

I looked at her. "Being black and speaking my truth," I said. "How about you?"

She burst out laughing. "That's funny. I've never heard anyone say that's the reason they were arrested in all my fifty-three years of living! But you really want to know what I'm in here for? I was arrested for conspiring to murder my husband. I discovered he was a two-timing cheat three weeks after the minute we both said *I do*. Turns out the so-called hit man I hired? He was an undercover cop."

I shook my head. "I'm sorry to hear that your marriage didn't work out."

"Well, I sure as hell ain't." She rose from the bed and got to her feet. "June, like the month," she said extending her hand.

I took a deep breath. "Lula."

June looked at me as her eyes locked onto mine. Her short natural hair was dyed blond and rolled into twists. Her irises and lids were bracketed with dark circles underneath. Standing at around five-seven, she looked like she weighed at least three hundred pounds. "I hope you either have a good lawyer, know how to fight, or have a direct speed line to talk to God. Because this is my second time being arrested," June said and shook her head. "Being locked in a cage like some wild animal? It's not something you ever really get used to."

"God willing, I actually don't plan to," I replied. "But I feel like I'm guilty until proven innocent."

June smiled at this. "You and a million other people! Listen I don't mean to be rude. But I was up all night because the crazy broad next to us *just had* to keep singing the national anthem. So I'm about to crash."

June then shuffled over to her bed, where she had lain down and eventually nodded off to sleep. I thought about my family, my friends, the soldiers in the Movement, and how I knew they would do everything within their power to help me. I thought about my life in reverse, and how, ironically, I'd found myself once again without any basic freedom. But I remembered my brethren, those forced against their will upon ships with names like *Desire*, *Isabella*, and *Jesus of Lübeck*, who'd been brought across the Atlantic to the New World. Those African slaves who had to endure more than I'd had to in my lifetime, more than I thought myself even capable.

I glanced at my watch and sauntered to the stainless steel sink in the room and washed my hands. Then I climbed up to my bunk, leaned my head against the cinder block wall and began to croon softly, the contemporary gospel song "Your Will," before falling asleep.

CHAPTER 14

I woke up in my cell at sunrise. I knew this because every morning I would wake at about the same time. It's funny how we take remedial things for granted, like being able to draw back a pair of curtains and have the sun bathe down our faces. Like hearing the cheerful chatter of birds when most of the world is filled with hate.

My usual daily routine consisted of fixing Mama and me something to eat before we ventured out into the world, hoping to make a difference. I glanced down at June who had fallen asleep with a copy of the Chicago Tribune lying over her face. She was snoring. There could have been a massive riot followed by a full-on lockdown, and I don't even think she would have noticed. For several

seconds she stirred before turning over on her right
side toward the wall.

Suddenly I heard familiar footsteps. It was a
sound I had gotten used to during the almost
twenty-four hours that I had spent here. It was the
same female officer who apparently had been
assigned to this wing of Division 4, which housed
women. I stood up as she stopped directly in front
of the cell. She inserted a key and opened the door.

"Come on. You're free to go."

"Me?"

"Whom else am I pointing to?"

I quickly gathered my shoes and my clothes that
I had worn when I'd first arrived. "What
happened?" I asked as I stepped out of the cell and
onto the catwalk.

"You got bail. And somebody's already posted it.
You're free to go, inmate," she said as she escorted
me toward a corridor. There was a several second
wait as the maximum-security gate buzzed open.

Together we walked through another corridor,
down a stairwell and toward the front of the building. The first group of people I saw was Ariel's
parents, another man whom I did not recognize,
Mama, Marcus, Ariel, and Tommy.

Mama opened her arms pulling me into her embrace. "Glad to see you get your freedom. I've been praying that God see to it, baby girl. See you free and able to go home."

As I remained locked in a hug with my mother, Randy cupped a hand on my shoulder. "I told you we'd get you out of here. Sorry it took this long." When I separated from hugging my mother, he gestured to the man on his left. "This is our family attorney, Jim Ernenwein, Lula. He was able to convince the judge presiding over your case to give you bail."

"Thank you," I told him. I looked around. "Thank *all* of you," I said as I took turns hugging everyone.

The attorney clapped a hand on Randy's back. "I'll be in touch. We'll confer again in a few days as I prepare for her next court date." He walked out of the building holding a leather briefcase.

"We still have an uphill battle against us. But it's a fight we're prepared to have. Our main concern is proving you and your mother's innocence, and finding out what happened to the Transporter," Randy said.

∾

Marcus, Mama and I stopped by L. Bowers, the elementary school where I worked so that I could talk to the school's principal, Gladys Brennan, about my absence. I was also told I had to fill out some papers regarding my time off. Basically, I was walking on thin ice and depending on the outcome of my case, didn't know if I'd have a job to come back to when everything was said and done. As soon as we left the principal's office, first-period classes were ending, and the kids charged out of their classrooms like they were running to open gifts on Christmas Day.

Malcolm Warner, the young and gifted art student who I had taken under my wing when he was bullied, ran up to me and wrapped his arms around my legs.

He glanced up. "I missed you Mrs. Darling. Where on earth have you been? I heard that you were on TV. That you might be in some kind of trouble."

I struggled with how to answer this question. I always taught my students that honesty was the best policy. So I searched for a tactful way to explain my absence.

"I had to spend time away for a cause that I believe in," I said and smiled.

Malcolm turned on his heel holding the straps of his backpack. "Oh, I see. Well, we're glad to have you back. Sorry, I have to go now." The three of us smiled as he hurried down the hall to his next class.

It was a joy seeing how much Malcolm had improved over time. He was now enrolled in an art class to further hone his talents, and his mother had been taking a more active role in his life. We exited the building and got into Marcus's SUV. He turned toward me as he started the engine. "We'll need to stop by the store to pick up some groceries. I promised you that when you were released I'd cook you, your mother, and Mama D. something really special." Marcus spread his hands. "I'm talking . . . a downtown, top-chef quality meal."

Mama laughed from the back seat. "Didn't know you knew how to cook, Marcus. What are you making?"

Marcus gripped the steering wheel as he pulled away and turned on the radio. "You'll see. I really wanted it to be a surprise, Ms. Darling." He nodded. "But she ain't fooling nobody. I think Lula already knows."

My mother looked at me. A smile bracketed her mouth. "What is it?"

I smiled back at her. "It could only be one thing." I swiveled my head toward the back seat. "There is one thing I know he's good at making, Mama. And that's Lasagna."

The three of us laughed.

When we got to Mama D.'s house, Marcus pulled up in the driveway on the side of the building. I helped him carry the groceries as we went up the porch and walked through the door.

"*Surprise!*"

I flashed a huge smile as I looked around Mama D.'s living room.

"Welcome home, Lula!"

My family and friends, even some of my coworkers had come by to wish me well. But I was even more shocked to see Pastor Tompkins, as well as our cousin, Joe Gatlin, here. Joe kindly muttered, 'excuse me' as he rolled his chair forward to greet me.

"Glad to see you home, Lula," he said grinning. "I tell everyone I know who use to run with me back in the sixties, that I know someone famous now. We had a running joke then that you weren't a real activist until you've been arrested. Welcome home cousin!" Joe announced as he extended his arms to hug me. It was good seeing him get out of the house and become more socially involved. Because Mama and I could never understand why he felt so obligated to be there, twenty-four seven, watching a bunch of kids whose grown parents lived under the same roof.

Pastor Tomkins walked over supporting himself with a cane. "Although I'm not a hundred percent, I wanted to be here for your welcome home party." He pointed. "I told you, Lord willing, I'm gonna be by your side when the going gets tough, and I meant what I said!"

I hugged him, and I hugged Ms. Mary, too. I was glad to see that Pastor Tompkins had recovered from his stroke and was able to leave his house. I imagined that he would soon be back in the pulpit giving one of his fiery sermons. This time with even more fire and brimstone than he'd given in the past.

"Thank you, everybody!" As I looked around the room, I was reminded that for every successful person who had ever achieved anything worthwhile, for every battle that was ever won, for every milestone made throughout history, there was often some unsung hero who helped to make it happen. I thought about how blessed I was to have the support of the people in this room. And so many more. Tears flooded my eyes. "This means a lot to me," I said and nodded appreciatively. Marcus grabbed some tissue, hugged me, then dropped a kiss on the crown of my head.

I smiled again as I composed myself. "We're not going to get all mushy up in here today. But know that I love and appreciate each and every one of you. Now let's eat. Because I haven't seen food this good since last week!"

Marcus turned on his record player and played his latest favorite anthem: "We're a Winner." As everyone mingled, I glanced at the table of food which Mama D. and Marcus had set up by the fireplace. There were the usual dishes one would expect when you had these many good cooks contributing in one house. Between Mama D. and Ms. Mary, they could have opened up a soul food restaurant and been the talk of all of Bronzeville, or better still, the talk of the entire South Side.

Later that evening when everyone was gone I sat on my living room couch with Marcus beside me. Mama was in her room giving us both our space and privacy. The only thing playing through my mind was a million and one questions about my case. When would I receive a court date and go to trial? How strong was the government's case against me? How skilled was Ariel's father's criminal defense attorney? And what would happen if I lose?

"I've been thinking about what I could do to help you," Marcus said as he ate some chips left over from the party. Then he turned to me. "I was wondering how we could take matters into our own hands. You know, like grab the bull by its horns."

"How do you mean?"

Marcus shifted on the sofa. "They think that Archibald dude might have the Transporter. And we know that *we* don't have it. So why don't we do what we can to try to find it ourselves? So we can clear your name and get you out of this mess."

I shook my head. "Marcus, if the government can't find it, what makes you think that we can?"

"Lula, the government has to go by the book. At least, I *think* they do. But that dude's probably got himself lawyered up to the point where they can't touch him without any concrete evidence."

"So you're saying that we should do something illegal? I'm not down with that, Marcus. I'm already in enough trouble as it is. You ever hear about the three strikes rule in Illinois? It means harsher punishment for repeat offenders. And I might already be on number two."

"Listen, you really want to know what I'm thinking?"

I nodded. "Please, enlighten me. Because the way you're talking we're all going to end up in jail."

"Okay. I propose that it's time for some *street* justice," Marcus said matter-of-factly.

"Street justice?"

"Yeah. Ever since the rally took place downtown, I've been keeping in touch with Darius. I had to thank him for what he did. Because of his close proximity, how he was able to quickly pull you off that stage. And I got to thinking that maybe he can play a role in this."

"Darius, the ex-felon?"

Marcus slowly nodded. "He's actually a really cool guy. Made a few mistakes in his life. But we seem to be on the same page whenever we talk. I think he can help us."

"How?"

Marcus reared back. "Well, I say we pay Mr. Archibald a visit. And let him know how important it is that we locate our property. With someone like Darius, and maybe the help of one of his friends, perhaps we can persuade Archibald to turn over the

machine if he still has it, by using a little intimidation tactic."

"Have you lost your mind?"

Marcus sat forward. "Lula, either we find what
happened to that machine, or you are going down
because of it. Now if that ain't intimidation, I don't
know what is! I'm not trying to lose you to the same
justice system that you're out there *fighting* against.
Look, I'll call up Darius, and we'll all go inside
Archibald's store together. Let's just see what
happens."

Several days later I saw firsthand just how serious
Marcus had been. Together we rode in his SUV
and met Darius along with one of his friends at the
corner of Chicago Avenue and North State Street.
Darius, with his jeans, leather jacket and ball cap
could have easily fit in during dinners at Mama D.'s
house or possibly even at Pastor Tompkins's church
on Sunday mornings. But the guy he'd brought with
him looked like someone you wouldn't want around
unless you were in imminent danger of having the
living crap beaten out you. The four of us walked in

front of a currency exchange at the busy intersection.

"Lula, Marcus, this is the homie, OG 12X. I've already briefed him on this whole thing and explained that we'll give him something for his troubles by the end of the week."

I waved as Marcus jerked his chin and then stepped forward. "I want to make it perfectly clear that we're only here to scare him," he said as he looked at Darius and his friend. "We just want our property back, nothing more than that. Are we clear?"

Darius and OG 12X nodded. "Yeah, we're clear."

The four of us headed toward the store. We had already called and pretended to be prospective buyers to find out when Archibald would be available. When we walked in, there was hardly any space to walk to the wood and glass counter, which was located straight ahead. On the walls and on shelves were oil paintings, ceramic or porcelain vases, antique wood clocks, and different types of furniture, some of which looked like relics from the antebellum South, and sat finely polished on the dark-tiled floor.

The man I believed to be Archibald, himself,

looked up. He appeared to be about fifty-something with a gray mustache and beard. His salt and pepper hair bracketed a bald spot on top of his head. He was wearing a black suit jacket over a royal blue shirt and a pair of dark jeans. He glanced up, startled. "Can I help you?"

Marcus stepped forward. "Yes, you can. We called on the phone about some old property," he said.

Archibald nodded. "I remember talking to you. Well, everything we have to sell is right here in the store." He came from behind the glass out onto the floor. "We're one of the largest dealers of antique and classic furniture in the Midwest. What type of piece are you looking for?"

"I'm gonna cut straight to the chase. You pulled my girlfriend's mother out of a piece of furniture out there on Chicago Avenue a while back. Well, as it turns out, that was a very valuable piece of equipment. Not only does it have sentimental value, but it's worth a lot to a lot of different people, including the United States government."

"I don't know what you're talking about."

Marcus rounded. "Sure you do. Because they have you on tape taking it. The FBI and the CIA came in here with a warrant and searched your place for it. And you seemed to have done a pretty good job of hiding it. But now we want it back. Because they're blaming my girl. They said you told them that she and her mother came in here and brought it from you for five hundred dollars, *cash*." Marcus shook his head, angered. "To make matters *worse*, my girl's mother was *homeless* when you found her out there on the street. You didn't even have the decency to help her. All you were concerned about was taking what didn't belong to you. So, we're going to ask you again, what did you do with it?"

Archibald raised a brow. "I no longer have it. I'm telling you the same thing I've told the authorities. And I need you to leave, right now." He took a step back. He looked to be assessing the situation and how to safely get out of it. I imagined that he probably had some type of silent alarm behind the counter. "Now I'm going to ask the four of you again, to leave, or I'm calling the police."

Darius shook his head. "You don't want to do that. I promise you, you don't want to go there, dude."

Archibald turned and started to walk behind the glass.

And that's when this whole plan of light intimidation went down the tubes.

OG 12X reached into his coat and produced a big black gun. He trained it on Archibald as the storeowner froze near the end of the counter. "You heard these people ask you where they property at. What? You think this here is a *game?* I eat fools like you for breakfast." He cocked his weapon. "Play-time is over! Now where it at?"

"Yo, X? What you doing, homie? We said no guns," Darius pleaded.

OG 12X kept his gun aimed at Archibald. "Nah, man. I got this, D. We done already asked this dude nicely. A fella like him don't understand how to take orders unless he's got a gun to his head."

As I stood in horror and watched this whole thing unfold, I began to wonder how it could possibly get any worse. Would Archibald be murdered? Shot to death in his shop? If so, I was going to wish this day had never happened. If so, I would be no better than the criminals I speak out against. In fact—everything that I had worked for, my absolute credibility—would all be wiped away if I were charged with being an accomplice to murder. I thought of the security cameras I'd been told had been monitoring the neighborhood. I glanced up at the ceiling and wondered if there were any cameras in here.

Archibald started to slowly raise his hands. "Just so you know I'm not trying to do anything funny," he said nervously. "I'll be honest with you. I know where it is. Once I found out how much it was worth and that the government was interested in it, I hid it."

"Where?" OG 12X yelled.

"In an abandoned warehouse on the south side. I figured no one would think to look for it there. Not something that valuable. It's in Englewood."

The four of us looked at each other in disbelief. "Englewood?" Marcus asked, stunned.

Archibald nodded his head. "Yeah. I know, right? That's precisely what makes it the perfect hiding place."

What I knew was that Englewood was among the most notorious areas in the city. There were times Mama and I had turned on the news to reports of multiple people being either shot or killed there. I wondered how was it that this white man dared to go into one of Chicago's roughest areas, with neither a badge nor a gun.

Darius walked to the front door, locked it, and pulled down the shades. "What's your name?"

"Herman. Herman Archibald."

Darius looked at OG 12X, then at Marcus and me. "All right, here's what we want from you, Herm. We want you to get your truck. Then we're going to take a ride out to Englewood so that my friends can get their property."

"Okay, but I need to get the keys." Archibald pointed. "They're right there in that jewelry box."

OG 12X walked over and firmly pressed the chunky metal gun into the side of the store owner's head. "Don't do anything funny."

Once Archibald removed the keys from the box the four of us walked out the back of the store. Outside, parked by itself at a loading dock was a large white box truck. "It's only room for two, three at the most," Archibald said as he kept his hands in the air.

"Me and X will ride in the truck. You all can follow us there in your car," instructed Darius.

Marcus and I walked to the corner where his SUV was parked in an outdoor parking garage. We got in, drove around, and then met up with and followed the rumbling truck as it pulled onto Chicago Avenue.

We arrived at the decaying two-story building within approximately forty minutes. Then we followed the truck into an old asphalt yard that had definitely seen much better days. The lot was covered with litter-strewn weeds, old truck tires, and was surrounded on three sides by a rusted chain-link fence. Archibald got out of the driver's seat. Darius, and then OG 12X quickly followed behind him. Archibald pointed at the warehouse and squinted. "That's the building right there. This is as close as we can get to it. We're gonna have to carry it out and then back to the truck."

We walked over strewn garbage on the ground. OG 12X kept his gun pressed directly into Archibald's side. I glanced up and saw that the structure had broken windows, falling gutters, and around its backside, a six-foot-wide opening where maybe a car had crashed into it.

We walked inside its cavernous space. There were pieces of wood and funky old mattresses everywhere. To our right was a homeless person hunched over a small fire trying to keep himself warm. "Don't worry, he's here all the time. He doesn't mess with anybody."

Archibald led us into an area that looked like it used to be some kind of room, maybe a basement. While keeping an eye out for anything unexpected, the four of us had to continually step over garbage and crumbled plaster, busted pipes, huge chunks of concrete. I glanced up and wondered if the crumbling ceiling above us now would cave. A moment later, I had to put a hand to my mouth at the site of several dead rats. Once further in, we went down some broken concrete stairs to a lower level. After studying the area, Archibald moved forward, leaned down, and slid some large wood paneling out of the way. Then he lifted a heavy burlap cover.

My eyes went wide as I stared at the machine that was responsible for me being here, no longer a slave. It was just as I had astonishingly remembered it. Marcus, Darius, and Archibald lifted it from beneath more burlap as my heart sank like a stone. There on the side of the Transporter, inscribed in large haunting letters, was Hartley Mansfield's name. I pulled out my phone and took a picture of it.

Marcus ran a hand over whatever material it had been made of back in Natchez. I imagined that neither Darius nor OG 12X had any idea that what they were looking at was actually otherworldly. I snapped several more photos. Suddenly, outside, the sound of loud rap music cut through the silence. "Who's that?" Darius looked at Archibald and asked.

The gray-haired man shrugged. "I have no idea," he said.

"All right. We got what we want. Let's get out of here," said Marcus, concerned.

Marcus, Darius, and Mr. Archibald lifted the machine and began to carry it up the stairs. OG 12X walked behind them with his gun carefully aimed at Archibald. As they made it to ground level, Archibald began to lower his side of the Transporter. Cords bulged at the base of his neck. "Listen, I'm out of breath," he said. "I need to take a break. Maybe, I'm not as young as you guys think I am."

OG 12X's eyes bugged like they were going to jump from their sockets. He quickly lunged forward pressing his gun at Archibald's temple. "*We don't have time to wait!* You need to keep it moving, fool!"

We waited for several long seconds. As Archibald got his wind, the three of them lifted the Transporter and began to move again. But suddenly, twenty feet in front of us five ominous figures entered the side of the building. They were dressed in hoodies, sagging pants to the point you could see the color of their underwear. Two were wearing knit skullcaps.

"What y'all doing here?" one of them yelled.

"We just came to get something that belongs to us," said Darius.

"What is it?" the guy shouted.

Archibald jerked his head forward. "It's just an old piece of furniture. An antique that we came to pick up for somebody."

"I don't believe that crap for one minute." The five of them began walking toward us. My heart started to beat in the back of my throat. I nervously thought that whatever was getting ready to happen, it was not good. I closed my eyes and quickly said a silent prayer. I wondered if this is where I would die, where they would bury me. I wondered if I would ever see my mama again. Because this is what happens when too much testosterone swirls in one place.

Darius, Archibald, and Marcus slowly lowered the Transporter on top of a bed of rubble.

The goon who had done all the talking reached into his waist belt and pointed a gun in our direction. "This is *our* territory. This whole *neighborhood* is our territory. So that means . . . anything found or buried here? It belongs to us!"

"Says who, fool?" OG 12X turned his gun from being pointed at Archibald and began to open fire. The gang members scattered and sought cover.

Marcus grabbed my arm and yanked me to the side of the building as Darius and Archibald bolted for the opening. As we ran, out the corner of my eye, I saw the homeless man attempt to escape. But he tripped and fell on whatever it was he'd used to ignite his fire, causing the flames to spread to a broader area.

Holding my phone, and with Marcus running beside me, we made it into the parking lot. In a desperate panic he reached into his pocket and hit the car's keyless remote to unlock its doors. I placed my hand on my knees and struggled to catch my breath, as did Marcus. When I looked up, the whole building had been engulfed in flames. "In a few minutes, this block will be crawling with cops and firemen. We need to leave, now!" he said.

As I climbed into Marcus's SUV, Darius came running pell-mell from around the corner. He opened the door and quickly jumped in the back-seat. "You okay?" Marcus asked him.

"Yeah. I'm good." Panting, Darius winced as he looked out the window. "Although I don't think my boy, X, made it. He got hit too many times," he said as he tried to catch his breath. "But I think ol' Herm made it out. I ain't never seen a white man run so fast. I saw him gunning his truck out the lot like he was at the Indianapolis Five Hundred."

Marcus started the engine and began to move forward. "Now before either of you talk to anybody about what happened here today, we need to make sure we're all on the same page. Do I make myself clear?"

I nodded. "Yes."

"Crystal," said Darius.

Marcus turned to me and met my gaze. "All right. Because this is only the first step in proving your innocence," he said.

CHAPTER 15

PASTOR TOMPKINS INVITED each of us to his church for a private dinner on Wednesday. Ms. Mary had been laboring all afternoon in the church's kitchen cooking up one of her trademark southern-inspired meals. Everyone who'd been a part of the Movement's inner circle had been invited to join us. Ariel's father had also requested that Jim Ernenwein attend to give an update on the government's pending case. I had learned later that Jim and Randy were very good friends and had played basketball together in college at Wisconsin State.

But the real reason Jim wanted to be there was that something was brewing regarding the feds, and their charges levied against me. I had been on pins and needles throughout the day wondering what he would have to say when we arrived. Would he be the bearer of some good news? Or would he announce that things had taken a turn for the worse? With a pending court date looming, my total freedom now hung in the balance.

With Mama by my side, we entered the church's dining room. We had been the last ones to arrive, but Ms. Mary made sure to put some food away.

Pastor Tompkins stood up from the end of the table, leaning to one side on his cane while beaming. "Two of my favorite ladies. Everyone has almost finished eating. But we made sure to save you some smothered chicken and rice—and everything nice," he mused, as he pulled Mama and me into his embrace with his right arm. "But first, let's go into my office and privately take care of business."

The six of us followed Pastor Tompkins into his office and sat down. I glanced near the middle of the table and watched as the attorney opened his briefcase. He took out some papers and then he met my gaze. "I almost didn't make it here in one piece. Some jerk in a BMW cut me off and nearly sent me veering into oncoming traffic," he said.

Pastor Tompkins offered a smile. "Well, with all

the expressway shootings we've had, you should count your blessings counselor."

Jim nodded. "That, I most certainly will."

The only thing the lawyer had been told was that the Transporter carried significant historical value, which was why the government wanted it in their possession. He laid out some papers before him on the table and looked directly at me. "Lula, I requested and was granted an emergency meeting with federal prosecutors. And with the evidence that I was able to present before them, including a sworn affidavit from firefighters that arrived on the scene, forensic evidence which was found among the charred remains, along with the photographs that you yourself took of the machine, they've agreed to drop all charges against you."

I nodded. Tears stood in my eyes. "Thank you," I said as I got up to give Jim a grateful hug. Everyone cheered and clapped. There was a collective feeling of relief, a positive spirit that had bonded us together like soldiers on the battlefield.

"It was apparent that Archibald had hidden the device all along. And that you and your mother were telling the truth the whole time. Herman Archibald has since been arrested and charged with perjury," Jim went on. His neatly trimmed brow shot up to his hairline. "A word of caution, though. If I were you, Lula, I'd try to remain low key for the time being. My suggestion is to stay far under the radar," he added.

"Okay," I replied. Mama reached over and hugged me as tight as she did the night we'd first been reunited. Locked in a tense embrace, we swayed side to side in our chairs, our cheeks pressed firmly together. She eventually let go, and we were now faced to face. "Don't let anyone tell you that prayer doesn't work!" she murmured as she thumbed away one of my tears.

As I took turns hugging Ariel and her parents and Marcus, I thought about how Mama and I had always found ourselves in a good place after going through one of life's many trials. I thought of my high school science class and how I was taught that a piece of carbon has to go through a process to become a diamond. Neither Mama nor I were perfect. But in our life's commitment in service to others, in our commitment to balancing the scales of injustice, we worked. We tirelessly worked so that a smile would emerge upon the face of God, a smile after he'd one day say, *Well done, thou good and faithful servant!*

We left out of Pastor Tompkins's office and then

went back into the dining area to join the rest of our group. They had been laughing and talking the whole time we were gone, courtesy of Pastor Mack's wild sense of humor.

"No charges!" I announced with my hands in the air. Everyone in the room cheered and clapped and stood up to congratulate me.

As I pulled out a chair for Mama, I glanced up and noticed Tommy walking through the door. He quickly came over and raised his arms to hug Ariel and then me. "Sorry I couldn't make it to the rally, Lula. My boss has been trippin' a lot lately," he called out as he took off his coat. "But I'm glad to know that you're okay. I'm also glad you're not gonna be charged." He looked at Marcus. "What would Ariel and I ever do without you two, huh?" Then he smiled. "You know how we do. We got to do *everything* together."

Everyone laughed. But then the mood turned to something else entirely. I watched as both Marcus and Tommy stood in front of us. They whispered back and forth for several seconds. Then they both got down on one knee.

"What are you doing? I asked.

They both reached into their pants pocket, pulling out small boxes. I looked at Ariel and gasped. There was a shudder of shock and gossip, as everyone else in the room suddenly paid attention.

Marcus smiled. "Lula, we've been together for a while now. We've been through a whole lot. And well, at this point? I couldn't imagine spending the rest of my life with anyone *but* you." He turned and looked at Tommy, whose cheeks had gone red. I glanced up and saw Ariel's parents walk slowly over, their hands clasped in front of them.

Tommy took a deep breath as he looked up. "Ariel, we've also been together for some time. We have our son together. And well, I think it's about time that we officially become as one. There's nobody else out there that I'd rather spend the rest of my life with."

Tommy and Marcus exchanged a nervous glance. Then they looked forward at Ariel and I. "So, with that said, ladies. Would you marry us?" they asked in unison.

"*Yes!*"

"*Yes!*"

My eyes widened as Marcus opened the small jewelry box revealing a sparkling diamond ring. He gently inserted it on my finger. Then he stood up, a smile spread across his face. I hugged him as he slowly spun me around. I watched as tears streamed down Ariel's face after Tommy placed the ring on her hand.

I turned toward my mother. "We're getting *married*, Mama!"

My mother put a hand over her heart and shook her head. "Congratulations, baby girl! I'm so happy for you!" Then she looked at Marcus. "You'll make a fine son in law, Marcus. Both of you are like two peas in a pod," she said. I looked on as Mama also congratulated Ariel and Marcus.

Ariel's parents came closer to congratulate the four of us. They both pulled the four of us into their embrace. "Congratulations girls! We love you both so very much," Patty said. She wiped away her falling tears.

Randy beamed with pride. "Today couldn't have brought a better smile on my face!" He gave Tommy a heartfelt hug. "Welcome to the family son."

Tommy nodded and grinned. "Thank you, sir. I'll definitely do right by Ariel and Thomas Jr."

"So, ladies, gentlemen, we've got an important announcement to make." Randy glanced at his wife. "As our gift to you, Patty and I are paying for everything. We're paying for you to have the double wedding that you've talked about in the past!"

Ariel and I both hugged her father as everyone smiled. "*Thank you!*"

Pastor Tompkins then hobbled over on his cane. "I'm glad that you young people have decided to do the right thing. There's not much out there in the streets anyway. Believe me, being a single man, I *know*." He raised his left arm and gestured across the room. "Mack, get over here and congratulate these young people on their engagement, will you?"

Pastor Mack came walking over holding a toothpick in his mouth. He was dressed in a two-piece maroon suit and black silk shirt. He looked like he'd added at least ten pounds since the last time we'd seen him. He furrowed his brow. "Who's tying the knot?"

"We are," the four of us blurted in unison and chuckled.

"Well, well. We're jumping the broom are we?" Pastor Mack pulled out a chair from a nearby table. "Have a seat young folks. I'd like to give you a few pointers before you stand before God on that glorious day and say, 'I do.' "

The four of us sat at the table with him. Marcus held my hand in his as we listened.

"Marriage is a big step, not to be taken lightly. But it's a beautiful thing when done properly. That being said, I have a few simple tips for you so that you may have a prosperous and blissful union." Pastor Mack's eyes darted back and forth between us. "Number one. Keep God first place in your life and in your marriage so that he will bless it. Two. You have to give each other space within the confines of your home. And be considerate of your spouse's feelings, interests, and whatnot. And lastly, please keep other people out of your business. Because not everyone has your best interest at heart. You ever hear the saying . . . misery loves company?"

"He's telling you what he knows from experience!" Pastor Tompkins cracked.

Pastor Mack nodded. "*Yessir*. My wife had a habit of listening to everyone else *but* me, the appointed head of the household. And when you've got two people who are not on the same page? Nine times outta ten it ain't gonna work. So we ended up getting a divorce in two thousand and twelve." He shifted his toothpick to the other side of his mouth. "However, enough with all that. I just want to say congratulations, and I pray that God blesses both your unions." He grinned and pointed. "Oh, and one other thing, if either of you ever wins the lottery, don't forget Pastor Mack gave you your first words of wisdom!"

Everyone broke into a shriek of laughter.

I looked around the room and was grateful that we could get together in good times instead of sad. Like at a funeral or a repast. Or at someone's bedside in the hospital. Or looking out of a cell wondering if you're ever going to see freedom again. This was one of the happiest moments of my life. I knew that Ariel and I would have a lot of planning to do in the days ahead. I also knew that with marriage and having a family, came increased responsibility and sacrifice.

I was ready for all of it.

~

Our day had finally come. And Mama and I arrived in a limo at 10 a.m. directly in front of the church. The driver got out and opened the door for us. "Congratulations. I hope your day goes well," he said.

I nodded. "Thank you." Then I glanced up at the front of the church. On the white sign, which hung from the building's brown brick exterior, and underneath: 1st Deliverance Baptist Church of Bronzeville, were the words, Congratulations on your nuptials: Lula and Marcus, Ariel and Tommy!

I smiled as Mama and I walked inside. Ms. Mary was the first one to greet us. "I hope you and Ariel are ready for your big day."

I nodded again. "I'm nervous, but I'm ready Ms. Mary. And thank you for all that you've done for us, including the church."

"You're welcome, Lula. The caterer said that they'd be at the banquet hall in an hour to set everything up."

"All right. Because I know after the ceremony people will be ready to eat."

Mama and I walked past Ms. Mary and peaked inside of the church. For several minutes I had to take everything in as I looked around. The sanctuary had been beautifully decorated in pink and white colors, with chiffon decorations at the end of each pew just as Ariel and I had envisioned it. There were beautiful bouquets of flowers sitting around the pulpit. I could smell their fragrance from where we stood.

Mama smiled and turned toward me. "You better start getting ready, Lula."

I walked toward the entrance of the church

and saw that several other cars had arrived outside. Climbing out of a silver Mercedes was our wedding coordinator, Tiffany. She was a friend of Ariel's mother and came highly recommended. Directly behind her were the Gatlins, including my cousin JuJu, his sister Shantay, and her daughter Takira, who we'd picked to be our flower girl.

I continued down the hall of the building, past Pastor Tompkins's office. I was ecstatic that he was in good enough health to officiate the ceremony for us. I opened the door to the church's bridal room and stood in the mirror. Tiffany, who was holding a white box that contained my wedding dress, immediately followed me inside. "Ariel should be here any minute. So far, everything is going according to schedule. How're you feeling, girl? You nervous?" she asked.

I turned toward her putting the cap on my lipstick. "Kinda, but with Ariel and I getting married together, it kind of makes things a little easier. A little less intimidating, if you know what I mean."

"Well, everyone in the bridal party should be here soon. The organist is on his way. And all the guests will hopefully be on time. Oh, and the DJ said that he's running a little late but will still be at the banquet hall in time to set up for the reception."

Suddenly the door swung open, and Ariel came charging through. "Sorry, I'm running behind. There was some kind of protest downtown, and my dad had to take another route. How ironic, right?"

I laughed. "Very, but at least you're here in enough time to make it down the aisle."

With the help of Tiffany and Shantay, Ariel and I put on our wedding gowns. Shantay, who had gone to cosmetology school, made sure that our makeup looked flawless. "You both look so beautiful," she said before she went to check on her daughter.

Afterward, Tiffany left the room to check on how things were going in the sanctuary. In the meantime, Ariel and I laughed and talked about how many kids we'd have. Where we would go on vacation for our ten-year anniversary.

We had so much in common and were able to agree on most everything, including where we were going for our honeymoon. And since Ariel had agreed with having the wedding at Pastor Tompkins's church—in turn, I agreed that Marcus and I would accompany her and Tommy on a double honeymoon in the coastal city of Puerto Vallarta.

There was a knock on the door. When Ariel opened it, I could hear "Spend My Life With You" playing throughout the building. Tiffany stuck her head inside the room. "It's about that time ladies."

I shot Ariel a nervous glance. We gave each other a quick hug. Then we were escorted down the hall where we met with her father, who was giving us both away.

Standing at the entrance to the closed doors of the sanctuary in a black tuxedo, he smiled and raised both elbows so that we could lock arms with him. Two of the church's staff persons opened the doors as the air rushed from my lungs. I nervously watched in amazement as everyone in the audience stood.

I glanced up, and as I stared forward, I saw Marcus and Tommy looking very handsome and dapper in their black tuxes. They stood in the pulpit beside Pastor Tompkins at the podium. I noticed the happy smiles and perfect attire on the Brides-maids and Groomsmen.

Slowly, the three of us walked down the aisle runner. The photographer we'd hired was directly in front of us. He steadily moved backward, snapping shots with a large black camera. Flashes of light filled the room as guests took pictures with their cell phones. Then, as the three of us neared the stage, two of the church's staff persons helped Ariel and I walk up the steps and onto the platform.

I looked at Marcus as he nervously wiped his head of perspiration. I stood directly in front of him, as Ariel stood in front of Tommy. "Please be seated," Pastor Tompkins instructed our guests. A woman briefly exited the sanctuary to take her crying baby into the hallway. "We are gathered here to witness the joining of not one, but two couples today in holy matrimony. I have the great pleasure of knowing each one of them personally. And I thank God for keeping them in the important work they do. Amen. Please let us bow our heads in prayer. Dearest God, we thank you for this opportunity to bless this marriage covenant. We ask that your presence bring unity to these hearts. Father God we ask that they walk with you, that they seek you each and every day. And in that, we know that all things will work together for the good of those that love you and are called according to your purpose."

"Who gives these women away?" the pastor asked.

"I do," said Randy, smiling proudly.

Pastor Tompkins put on a pair of black-rimmed

glasses. Then he opened a bible that was lying on the podium before him. "Please pull out the bibles in front of you and go to Ephesians chapter 5, verse 22." After reading Scripture, he asked that Marcus and Tommy pull out the wedding bands and place them on our hands. Tears filled my eyes as each of us repeated a pledge to the other, to honor, to cherish, and obey. I glanced over as Tommy held Ariel's hands, then looked at Marcus as he held mine. Pastor Tompkins pulled his microphone closer and briefly addressed the four of us. "Marriage is not to be taken lightly. For it is a holy union ordained by God. Marriage is such that you become entwined as one. One family. One faith. And one flesh. Proverbs 18:22 says, 'He who finds a wife finds a good thing, and receives favor from the Lord.' And for as much as Marcus and Lula, and Tommy and Ariel, have consented in holy wedlock, and have witnessed the same by the joining of the hands, by the taking of solemn vows and the exchanging of rings in the presence of God's sight, and before this company as a minister of the gospel of the Lord Jesus Christ, before God and witnesses here today, it is my dutiful pleasure to pronounce both couples, as husband and wife." He smiled. "Gentlemen, you may kiss your brides."

Marcus leaned forward and gave me the sweetest kiss ever. Ariel and I turned and held up our flower bouquets smiling. There was cheering and clapping throughout the room. Pastor Tompkins looked out into the audience. "It is my esteemed pleasure to present to you for the first time, Mr. and Mrs. Marcus Whitaker, and Mr. and Mrs. Thomas Rayome!" The cheering and clapping resumed. Suddenly, "No One" by Alicia Keys played through the church's speakers. Staff members came up on both sides of the stage and escorted us from the pulpit. Then we stood in the center aisle and waved at our guests.

As I shook hands and said hello, Ariel and I heard a number of well wishes. " 'God bless you! Congratulations. You look so radiant, so happy and beautiful!' " I immediately hugged my mother who was sitting in the first row. "Love you, baby girl. I wish nothing but a lifetime of happiness for you and for Marcus," she said beaming. Mama D. struggled to stand next to Mama. So Marcus leaned over and held her arm to help her maintain her balance. Once on her feet Mama D. delightfully nodded her head.

"Congratulations newlyweds. All I have to say is . . . you know I'm up in age. So please don't wait too long to give me some great-grandchildren," she said.

"We won't," I told her and smiled. I looked at her and Mama. "So how'd you both enjoy the ceremony?"

Mama D. grinned. "Oh, honey. It was *so* beautiful. Marcus and all the men looked so handsome. And the ladies looked so pretty. When all is said and done, I want a great big picture to hang over the mantle in my living room!"

"Everything was lovely and went along without a hitch. Pastor Tompkins did an outstanding job, especially considering his health," my mother said.

We continued down the aisle to greet our guests. And as we got near the back of the church, I noticed the smile on Marcus's face suddenly disappear. I looked forward to seeing what he was staring at. A woman walked toward us holding a small purse. She had a honey-caramel complexion and close-cropped hair. A small scar was noticeable on her right cheekbone. She was wearing jeans and a turquoise blouse. And her face looked weathered by a hard life, stress, or both. "Hello Marcus," she said shyly.

"What are you doing here?" Marcus replied.

She took a deep breath and looked around. "I

know what you must think of me. Because I've been absent for a very long time. And I deserve whatever opinion you have about me. But I couldn't miss my only child's wedding. And . . . more importantly, I wanted to tell you how truly sorry I am. And to ask for your forgiveness." My eyes widened in shocked disbelief.

Out of the corner of my eye, I saw Pastor Tompkins escorting Mama D. toward the back of the sanctuary. They were coming up directly behind us. Then I watched as Mama D. stopped several feet away, in slack-faced shock. "Demetria?" she muttered, squinting her eyes as if processing what she had seen was real.

"Hello Mama," the woman said extending her hand.

"Oh, my Lord. How are you?"

The woman nodded. "I'm fine Mama."

"How did you find out about—"

"I've kept my ears to the street, and actually heard about the wedding several months ago." The woman looked down, apparently embarrassed. Then she glanced up. "Well, I didn't want to spoil your wedding by just showing up uninvited. So, I think I'll just leave now."

"*Hold on!*" Mama D. blurted. "Girl, you've been

gone all these years?" She shook her head. "It's time you stop hiding from your problems . . . your family —and face reality. It's time you turn your *life* around, Demetria."

Demetria exhaled deeply and smiled. "Your point is valid Mama. You get absolutely no argument from me. Because despite my shortcomings, my downfalls, I always knew he was in good hands and would turn into a fine young man." She shifted her gaze to my husband. "Well, Marcus, aren't you going to introduce me to your new bride?"

"Lula, this here is . . . my mother, Demetria Whitaker."

Demetria reached out her hand. "Nice to meet you, Lula. I hope to get to really know you one day."

"Nice to meet you, too." I looked at Marcus, and then at his mother. "I look forward to getting to know you as well."

Marcus borrowed a pen and a piece of paper from one of the guests. "Here's the address to where the reception is being held. Hopefully, you can make it."

His mother nodded. "Thank you." Tears flooded her eyes. She waved, turned and then walked out of the church.

Suddenly Darius came over. He was wearing a blue pinstriped suit, and his hair was neatly styled in short dreads. Standing by his side was a petite woman I presumed was his date. "I just wanted to say congratulations," he said extending his hand. "And I wanted to thank you and Pastor Tompkins for really looking out—when most people would've given up on me."

I pulled him into my embrace. "You're welcome." Then I glanced at him and his companion. "Are you both coming to the reception? It's going to be off the charts. Jay Killa will be performing as a gift to Marcus."

Darius shrugged. "Nah, unfortunately, I won't be able to make it. Because, actually, I have to be at work in a couple of hours. I got a job working at a distribution center in Plainfield."

"That's truly a blessing, Darius! Glad to hear that things are looking up," I said beaming. "Just goes to show there *are* such things as second chances."

Darius nodded. "I know, right?" He looked at his date. "Well, it's about time we bounce. But I hope everyone has a good time tonight at the reception."

"We will, bro. Sorry you can't make it," Marcus said as he hugged his friend.

They parted and were now face-to-face. Darius quickly reached up and slapped a backhand on Marcus's chest. "Hey, don't get too drunk. You know how you get when you and Killa hang out," he said laughing.

And just as quickly as he had appeared he was gone.

The rest of the wedding party proceeded out onto the sidewalk. There was a row of white limousines waiting patiently at the curb. Several drivers stood with their car doors open as they talked on their phones. Some of the Bridesmaids and Groomsmen had already climbed inside and were singing "All of Me" by John Legend. Lifting my dress, I turned to look for Ariel, Tommy, and her parents. I wanted to thank them for making this day one that I would cherish forever. Through the church's opened doors I looked into the sanctuary and noticed them taking some last minute pictures.

Then for a brief moment, I looked up at the sky. The sun's rays washed over me as I tilted my head to the clouds. I imagined that not only God was looking down, but the ancestors had been too. The ones who died with only a prayer that their

suffering had not been in vain. That future generations would somehow, some way be better. I believe
I saw them this day, their spirits appearing like
manna from heaven. They are the angels watching
over me.

ABOUT THE AUTHOR

ALEX DEAN is the author of *the Alexis Fields Thrill* series and the *Lula Darling* series. He is an entrepreneur, former musician, and somewhat of a health enthusiast who enjoys being creative. He writes thrillers as well as other sub-genres of fiction and lives in Illinois with his family. For previews of his upcoming books and more information about Alex Dean, please visit alexdeanauthor.com.

Word-of-mouth is crucial for any author to succeed. **If you enjoyed this book, please consider leaving a review, even if it's only a line or two; it would make all the difference and would be greatly appreciated**.

To receive special offers, bonus content, & news about Alex Dean's latest books, **Sign Up** for his Newsletter today!

ACKNOWLEDGMENTS

I would like to thank God for His many blessings, a heartfelt thanks to my wife and my parents for their valuable feedback, my children and family for their love and support. A big thanks to my in-laws for supporting my endeavors, and a tremendous thanks to my readers for your continued support.

Made in the USA
Lexington, KY
23 August 2018